Sharon Kendrick

BEDDED
FOR REVENGE

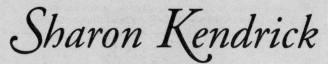

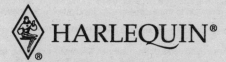
HARLEQUIN®

TORONTO • NEW YORK • LONDON
AMSTERDAM • PARIS • SYDNEY • HAMBURG
STOCKHOLM • ATHENS • TOKYO • MILAN • MADRID
PRAGUE • WARSAW • BUDAPEST • AUCKLAND

ISBN-13: 978-0-373-12591-3
ISBN-10:   0-373-12591-7

BEDDED FOR REVENGE

First North American Publication 2006.

Copyright © 2006 by Sharon Kendrick.

This edition published by arrangement with Harlequin Books S.A.

www.eHarlequin.com

Printed in U.S.A.

All about the author…
Sharon Kendrick

When I was told off as a child for making up stories, little did I know that one day I'd earn my living by writing them!

To the horror of my parents I left school at sixteen and did a bewildering variety of jobs: a London DJ (in the now-trendy Primrose Hill!), a decorator and a singer. After that I became a cook, a photographer and, eventually, a nurse. I waitressed in the south of France, drove an ambulance in Australia, and saw lots of beautiful sights, but could never settle down. Everywhere I went I felt like a square peg—until one day I started writing again and then everything just fell into place.

Today I have the best job in the world: writing passionate romances for Harlequin. I like writing stories that are sexy and fast-paced, yet packed full of emotion; stories that readers will identify with and that will make them laugh and cry.

My interests are many and varied: chocolate, music, fresh flowers, bubble-baths, films, cooking and trying to keep my home from looking as if someone's burgled it! Simple pleasures—you can't beat them!

I live in Winchester and regularly visit London and Paris. Oh, and I love hearing from my readers all over the world…so I think it's over to you!

With warmest wishes,

Sharon Kendrick (www.sharonkendrick.com)

To Michele et Claude Bertrand,
for their wonderful hospitality and for
showing me a different side of glorious Paris.

CHAPTER ONE

CESARE DI ARCANGELO'S eyes narrowed as he watched the woman begin to walk down the aisle, looking as though butter wouldn't melt in her beautiful mouth, and he found he wanted to crush it, lick it, bite it, eat it.

Yet he felt the flicker of a pulse at his temple and was aware of the faint wash of disappointment—for he had wanted to feel nothing, to remain as coolly indifferent as women always accused him of being. But as she approached, in a cloud of silk-satin and lace, that hope shattered within him. He felt anger rise like poison in his blood, but something else too. Something more powerful still—which it seemed that all the years could not diminish. Something which had kept the human race going since the beginning of time.

Lust.

And maybe that was better—because if lust was a problem then it had a pretty simple solution.

The sound of the organ music was building up to a crescendo, and the heavy scent of the flowers was in-

toxicating, but all Cesare could see from his seat near
the back was Sorcha, smiling, her bouquet held in front
of a waist which was as sensuously narrow as it had
been when she was just eighteen.

What a gorgeously sexy bridesmaid she was…

Feeling the hard, heavy tug of an erection straining
against the exquisitely tailored trousers of his morning
suit, Cesare briefly clenched and then flexed his hands,
willing the hard throb of desire to disappear.

He had slid into his seat at the back of the church at
the very last minute. It had been a low-key but deliberate lateness—for the sight of Cesare di Arcangelo tended
to create interest and excitement wherever he went.

Mega-rich, sexy Italians seemed to be on the top of
everybody's wish list. It was why the hottest hostesses
in all the major cities in the world pursued him with the
fervour of astronomers who had just discovered a brand-
new planet.

He scanned the congregation for Sorcha's mother.
Yes. There she was—in a hat as big as the Sydney
Opera House—and even from this distance it was easy
to read the cat-got-the-cream satisfaction of her body
language. She must be very pleased—for a rich son-in-
law spelt hope for a family firm beset with problems.
Would Emma's new husband be willing to pour the
necessary funds into the family business to keep cred-
itors at bay?

Cesare doubted it. Money only worked up until a
certain point—after that, you might as well hold it up to

the winds and let it scatter. Problems had to be fixed; they couldn't be patched up. His mouth twisted. All problems.

The bride and groom were now passing, but he barely gave them a glance. Nor the parade of chubby little bridesmaids, or the scowling pageboys clad in satin romper suits which they would never forgive their mothers for forcing them to wear.

No, it was the only adult bridesmaid, with the bright, strawberry blonde hair woven with tiny rosebuds, who commanded his total, undivided attention. She was his problem—the unfinished business which he needed to put to bed. Beautiful Sorcha Whittaker, with the green eyes, and the bright hair like a waterfall, and a body as supple as an eel.

He had her trained in his sights, like a hunter with his prey fixed—for he wanted to see her reaction when their eyes met for the first time in… How long was it now? A pulse began to beat at his temple. Seven years? A minute? An eternity?

He saw her knuckles tense and her footsteps falter so much that for a second she almost came to a halt. Time froze as he stared into eyes as green as a rainwashed woodland and saw the confusion and consternation which flew into them as she stared straight back.

Cesare watched her face blanch and her lips tremble and felt a fleeting moment of utter triumph—swiftly followed by frustration that he could not just take her there and then.

If only this were not a crowded place of worship.

How much easier if they were alone and he could swiftly remove all the underwear hidden beneath the canopy of that monstrous dress—could swiftly obliterate desire and frustration with sweet release.

And then just walk away.

For a moment he was powerless—as once she had made him powerless all those years ago. But soon she would have fulfilled her role as bridesmaid, and then he would take the power back with relish.

'Bride or groom?' asked the delicious-looking brunette in banana-coloured silk who was standing beside him.

Cesare swallowed, for his erotic thoughts had inevitably made him ache. He flicked his eyes over the brunette, who widened hers so provocatively that she might just as well have had *Yes, please!* tattooed on her forehead. 'Groom,' he answered drily. 'And you?'

'Mmm. Me, too. He said there were going to be some gorgeous men here, and by heck—he wasn't lying!' The brunette batted her eyelashes quite outrageously. 'Any chance I could cadge a lift to the reception?'

Cesare's mouth hardened into a smile. 'Why not?'

Outside the church, Sorcha was standing in the wedding group while it seemed as if a thousand photos were being taken. But her smile felt as if someone had slashed it across her face with a razor.

Her eyes flickered over to the tiny church and she saw a tall, broad-shouldered figure emerging, having to bend his head to avoid bumping it on the low door, and her heart felt as if someone had ripped open her chest and squeezed it with a bare fist.

Cesare!

Here!

'Sorcha! This way! Look at the camera!'

With an effort she tore her eyes away from him and a flashbulb exploded in her face, temporarily blinding her. When it cleared he had gone. But there was her brother, Rupert, standing in a group, and she hurried over to him, completely ignoring the appreciative comments which came from his fellow ushers. Her mouth was dry and her heart was beating like a drum. And it hurt. It shouldn't do, but it hurt.

'Who in their right mind invited Cesare di Arcangelo today?' she managed, though her specially perfected chief bridesmaid smile didn't waver.

'Oh, he's here, is he?' Rupert looked around and an odd expression came into his eyes. 'Good.'

'Good?' Sorcha tried to squash all the instinctive fears which came scurrying to the forefront of her mind. Because none of them might be true, and it was her sister's wedding day, after all.

It was supposed to be a happy occasion, a joyous day—like all weddings should be. And it had been—right up until the moment when she had seen Cesare's dangerously handsome face and had felt her heart clench as if it was making up its mind whether to beat again.

Just the sight of his brilliant black eyes had taken her

back to another time and another place—and mocked her with the lesson she had been learning ever since. That no other man could ever match up to him. And one look at him had reminded her exactly why.

Her mouth was dry and her breath was rapid, but she sucked in a deep breath and tried to stay calm. 'Rupert, did you know he was going to be here?'

There was a pause. 'Er…kind of.'

'*Kind* of? And so did Emma, presumably—since she's the bride?'

'Yeah. Ralph's family does a lot of business with di Arcangelo. You know that, Sorcha.'

Yes, she knew that—but it was one of those things you knew and kept pushed to the back of your mind. The same way that you knew natural disasters occurred, but you just didn't spend your time thinking about them until you had to. 'And it didn't occur to any of you to have the decency to tell me he'd been invited, in view of our…our *history?*'

Rupert looked vaguely bored. 'You went out with him a few years ago—what's the big deal? And anyway—he asked me not say anything. He wanted it to be a surprise.'

She wanted to yelp—*What do you mean, he asked you not to? I am your sister, and as such I take precedence over Cesare di Arcangelo—in spite of his affluence and influence.*

'Oh, it's certainly a surprise,' said Sorcha lightly—but if she said any more then Rupert would think she cared. And she didn't. Not any more. She had to get things into perspective. Cesare was simply part of her past who would soon be gone, if not forgotten.

But why was he here? What possible reason could there be for re-establishing a family connection which had fizzled out years ago? Loyalty to her brother? Had they really been that close? Or was it just what it seemed—he was attending the wedding of a son of a business colleague?

It was like being caught in a trap which no one apart from Sorcha could see. Even though the sun was shining, and the church was picture-postcard perfect, and the bells were pealing out, inside she felt a bleak pang of regret. Time healed, that was what everyone said—and now it seemed that the rest of the world had been colluding in a great big conspiracy of lies.

But she played her part to the maximum and flashed a series of bright, happy smiles for the cameras until they wanted just couple shots of the bride and groom and she could escape.

She just wasn't sure where.

With an odd kind of sixth sense, Sorcha suddenly became aware of being watched as surely as if eyes were burning into her back, branding her pale skin through the delicate silk-satin of her bridesmaid dress. And—try as she might—she couldn't stop herself from turning round to see, even though she knew exactly who it was.

This was the true meaning of the word *irresistible,* she thought as she tried uselessly to pull against the power he exerted. As if she were a snake and he some charmer, summoning her against her will. And she looked round to find herself dazzled by the ebony gaze of Cesare di Arcangelo.

Stay away, Sorcha prayed silently—but her prayer went unanswered. Sunlight bouncing off his gleaming blue-black hair, he walked across the church path towards her, tall and dark and supremely confident—leaving a sulky-looking woman in a bright yellow dress glaring at his retreating back.

Sorcha felt a lump in her throat—as if someone had rammed in a pebble large enough to block her windpipe—and she briefly closed her eyes, imagining—almost praying—that she would pass out. What a merciful release that would be. To faint and discover when she opened her eyes again that Cesare had gone—as if he had never set foot here in the first place. Almost as if she had dreamt it all up.

But she did not faint, and there was no mercy. Or dream. Instead, the air came flowing back into her lungs as she stared back at him—and just the sight of him was the visual equivalent of a punch in the solar plexus.

'Cesare,' she said, and it came out as a whisper.

He was wearing a pale, formal suit in grey, made from some expensive fabric which hung and hugged his muscular body in all the right places. Whoever had designed it must have decided that hinting at a man's raw sexuality was the way to go—or maybe it just had something to do with the man who was wearing it.

The grey contrasted with jet-dark hair which was thick and silky-straight—just like the outrageously thick black eyelashes which shielded eyes as rich as dark chocolate. He looked more like an international sex symbol than the millionaire entrepreneur he really was—who had taken the long-established wealth of the di Arcangelo family, transformed it into super-riches and made himself into a bit of a legend in the process.

Everything about him was perfect—even that slightly restless expression on his face, and the cold and quizzical eyes that hinted at an intellectual depth which lay beneath the charismatic exterior. She had once thought that it wasn't possible for a man to be as gorgeous as Cesare, but somehow he had defied the improbable—and seven years had only added to his striking physical impact.

Somehow she managed to pull herself together—even though there was still some remnant of the lovestruck girl inside her who wanted to wrap her arms around his neck and pull his gorgeous face down to kiss her, wriggle her untutored body restlessly against the hard perfection of his.

Her heart was hammering, but somehow she inclined her head politely—so that to the casual observer it would look as though the chief bridesmaid were greeting just another guest.

'Well,' she said coolly. 'This is a surprise.'

'Don't you like surprises?' he murmured.

'What do you think?'

He smiled as he sensed the tension in her. 'Ah, Sorcha,'

he murmured, his gaze travelling with slow insolence over the body of the only woman who had ever rejected him. '*Bene, bene, bene*—but how you've grown, *cara.*'

She wanted to tell him not to look at her like that—but that wasn't entirely true, and she didn't want to be branded a hypocrite. Because even while she despised that blatantly sexual scrutiny, wasn't there some traitorous part of her body which responded to it?

She could feel it in the soft throbbing of her pulses and in the uncomfortable prickle as her breasts thrust against the lace brassière she wore—as if her nipples were screaming out to be touched. And Cesare would have noticed that. Of course he would. Once, in that protective way he'd had with her, he would have defused the sexual tension. But not any more. Now he was just taking his time and enjoying it.

And the time for social niceties was past. She had to protect herself. She had to know the truth.

'What the hell are you doing here?' she demanded.

Black brows were arched. 'What an appalling way to speak to an invited guest, *cara,*' he answered silkily. Because now was not the time to tell her. *Non ora.* He was going to savour the timing of this, to maximise the impact when he dropped his bombshell straight into her beautiful lap. 'Didn't you know I was coming?' he questioned innocently.

'You know very well I didn't—since my brother says you left instructions for it to be kept all hush-hush!' Sorcha fixed him with a questioning look, reminding herself that this was *her* territory and that he was definitely trespassing. 'So why all the cloak and dagger stuff? Do you want to be a spy when you grow up, Cesare?'

He gave a soft, appreciative laugh—for opposition always heightened the senses. He thought how much more spirited she had become with the passing of the years, and oh, but he was going to enjoy subduing that fire. 'Why? Do you think I'd make a good one?'

'No. You'd never blend into a crowd,' she retorted, before realising that although it was the right thing—it was also the wrong thing to say. It might have sounded like a compliment, and that was the last thing she wanted. 'Why didn't you warn me?'

'Maybe I knew how much you would have opposed my being here,' he observed.

'You were right.'

'And maybe I wanted to see your face when you did. To see your first genuine reaction. Do you remember the last time we saw one another, my *love?*'

In spite of the sarcasm which dripped from it, the word made her heart clench. Until she reminded herself that it was a redundant word as far as they were concerned—as unreal as everything else about their relationship. The engagement that never was, the happy-ever-after which never happened. How could something which had never really existed, have hurt so much?

She gave him a blank look. 'I don't believe I do.'

'Liar,' he said huskily, black eyes sliding over the tight aquamarine silk bodice and the exuberant thrust of her pert breasts. His gaze lingered long against the tiny tips of her nipples, which looked so startlingly sharp against the shining material, and he wished that he could take his tongue to them. 'Do you remember how it felt to be in my arms and to have my tongue inside your mouth? Are you regretting now that we didn't ever get around to having full sex?'

She flinched as if he had hit her. As if he had led her down a predictable path and she had failed to see where it was heading—except that Cesare had never been explicit like that with her before.

Yet she was letting his words wound her, and she was in danger of making a fool of herself. People were already starting to turn round to look at them—as if the almost tangible tension between them was setting them apart. Murmured questions were buzzing around the high-society guests, and Sorcha's gaze darted around to meet frankly curious stares.

His black eyes followed hers. 'Do you suppose they're thinking what an attractive couple we make?' he murmured. 'Do you suppose that they are imagining the contrast of your pale skin being pinned down by the darkness of mine? Are you imagining it too, *cara mia,* just as I am? Do you think that they would be disappointed if they knew the reality of our lovemaking?'

Her pulse rocketed. 'Cesare—stop it. Just *go*. Please! Why are you doing this?'

This was better, much better. Her lips parting in breathless appeal, her eyes darkening at his erotic taunt.

With a cruel pleasure which excited him, Cesare continued to play with her as a cat would a helpless mouse. 'What a way to greet the man you once claimed to adore.'

Sorcha felt the blood rushing to her ears so that they were filled with a roaring sound, like the ocean. 'I was young and stupid then,' she said hoarsely.

'And now?'

'Now I'm old enough to realise the lucky escape I had.'

'Well, then, we are agreed on something at least,' he answered evenly.

Sorcha hesitated. Maybe she had got him all wrong. Maybe he wanted to make peace. Maybe… She peered over his shoulder to where the brunette in the biliously coloured outfit was still standing staring at him and her heart pounded. 'Is that your…girlfriend?'

He heard the acid tone in her voice even though she did her best to disguise it, and turned his head to glance over at the woman, who wiggled her fingers at him in a wave. 'Sindy?' He gave a slow smile. 'Jealous, Sorcha?'

'Not at all.' But she was lying, and Sorcha wondered if Cesare realised that. She found herself wanting to lash out like a little cat—to say that the woman's skin was sallow, that she was wearing the wrong colour, that she was not fit to be his girlfriend. But that was all wrong— she shouldn't be feeling this way. Not now.

'Have you spoken to my mother?'

'Not yet. I'll catch up with her at the reception.'

Sorcha froze. 'You're coming to the reception?' she whispered.

Cesare smiled. This was better than he could ever have anticipated! 'You think I have flown all the way from Rome to hear a couple repeat a set of vows which will probably be broken before the year is out?' he questioned cynically. 'I may not be a big fan of weddings, but nobody can deny that they offer an opportunity to indulge in some of the more pleasurable aspects of life. And I shall look forward to being back in your house.'

The black eyes glittered in a way which took her right back to forbidden territory—more emotional than erotic, and all the more dangerous for that.

'Shall we dance together later, Sorcha?' he finished. 'Perhaps even go for a swim, just like the old days—*si?*'

But the old days were gone—long gone. She wanted to convince herself that the person she was then had been markedly different—so that if the younger Sorcha had walked up and said hello she wouldn't be able to recognise her. And yet while in many ways she *was* different—in others she felt exactly the same. Why else would there be such a dull ache in her heart when she looked at the man she had believed herself to be in love with?

'I would tell you to go to hell,' she said slowly, 'if I didn't think you'd already taken up a permanent berth there!'

'Why? Do you want to come and lie in it with me?'

His soft mocking laughter was still ringing in her ears as Sorcha pushed her way through the crowds to where a dark limousine was waiting to whisk the bridesmaids and pageboys back to the reception. Four young faces pressed anxiously against the glass as Sorcha gathered up armfuls of tulle and silk and levered herself in next to them.

The bridegroom's niece scrambled onto her lap and planted a chubby finger right in the middle of her cheek.

'Why are you cryin', Sorcha?'

Sorcha sniffed. 'I'm not crying. I just got a speck of dust in my eyes.' She dabbed a tissue at her eye and then beamed the worried child the widest smile in her repertoire. 'See? All gone!'

'All gone!' they chorused obediently.

Sorcha bit her lip and turned it into another smile. How simple it was to be a child in a world where things vanished just because an adult told you they had. The monster under the bed had gone away because Mummy said so.

But memories were like those childhood monsters— always lurking in dark places, waiting to capture you if you weren't careful. And some memories burned as strongly as if they had happened yesterday.

CHAPTER TWO

SORCHA had met Cesare di Arcangelo the summer she'd turned eighteen, the hottest summer for decades. It had been the year she'd left school and the year most of her classmates had finally rid themselves of the burden of their virginity—but Sorcha had not been among them. Her friends had laughed and called her old-fashioned, but she'd been holding out for someone special.

But that summer she had felt as ripe and ready as some rich fruit ready for picking—and hormones had bubbled like cauldrons in her veins.

She'd arrived home from a final school trip to France on a baking hot day with a sky of blinding brightness. There had been no one to meet her at the station, and no reply when she'd phoned the house, but it hadn't particularly bothered her. She'd had little luggage, and because it was beautiful and so green, and so *English* after the little mountain village of *Plan-du-Var,* she had decided to walk.

The air had been unnaturally still and the lane dusty,

but the sky had been the clearest blue imaginable—with birds singing their little hearts out—and suddenly Sorcha had felt glad to be home, even if she was slightly apprehensive about the future.

Up until that moment everything had been safely mapped out for her—but with the freedom which came from leaving school came uncertainty too. Still, she had worked hard, and she'd been offered a place at one of the best universities in the country if her exam results were as good as had been predicted.

She'd approached the house by the long drive—the honey-coloured mansion where Whittakers had lived since her great-great-grandfather had first got the bright idea of marketing his wife's delicious home-made sauce. From humble terraced house beginnings, her great-great-grandma's unique recipe had become a national institution, and soon enough money had poured in to enable him to satisfy his land-owning longings and buy himself a real-life stately home.

But of course that had been in the days before a croissant or a bowl of muesli had become staple breakfast fare—in the days when a full fry-up with Whittaker Sauce had been the only way to start the day. The slow, gradual decline in the family fortunes had soon begun, but it had been so slow that you didn't really notice it, and it was much easier to ignore something if it just crept up on you.

Sorcha had given a small sigh of satisfaction as she'd looked towards the house, because in that moment it hadn't looked stately, it had just looked like home. From this far away you didn't really notice that the walls were crumbling and the roof needed replacing, and of course in the summer months it really came into its own.

Come winter and there would be so much frost on the inside of the windows you could write your initials in it and see the steam of your breath as it rushed out against the cold air. Anyone else might have capitalised on the house's assets and sold it, but not Sorcha's mother, who was hanging on to it with grim determination.

'It's a huge asset,' Mrs Whittaker always pronounced, and no one could argue with that. Rural it might look—but a few miles beyond its expansive grounds lay a road which took you straight into London in less than an hour.

Pushing open the oak front door, Sorcha had gone inside to an echoing silence, where dust motes had danced in the beams of sunlight which flooded in through the stained glass. She'd seen a man's cashmere sweater lying on one of the chairs—beautiful and soft in palest grey—and raised her eyebrows. A bit classy for Rupert! Her brother must have given himself a pay rise.

The house had been empty—so she'd gone up to her bedroom, with its schoolgirl echoes of prizes—rosettes won at horseriding and shiny silver cups for swimming.

From there she could see the pool, and to her astonishment she'd seen that it had been cleared—instead of turgid green water with leaves floating on it like dead lilies it was a perfectly clear rectangle of inviting aquamarine.

Pulling open a drawer, she'd found a swimsuit and

squeezed herself into it—she must have grown a lot since last year. Overnight, she'd seemed to go from being a beanpole of an adolescent to having the curvy shape of a real woman. She was going to have to go shopping.

The water had felt completely delicious as she'd dived in and begun to swim, length after length of slicing crawl, each stroke taking her further and further into a daydream. She'd been so wrapped up in her thoughts that she hadn't noticed the man who was standing there until she had come up for breath, exhausted, sucking in the warm summer air as the water streamed down her hair in rivulets.

Sorcha had started. For a moment all she'd registered was jet-dark hair and silken olive skin, but as she'd blinked the water out of her eyes she'd seen that it was a stranger—and a disturbingly handsome stranger, to boot.

In a pair of faded jeans and an old black T-shirt, he'd looked like one of the gardeners her mother employed to try and make a dent in the overgrowth at the beginning of every season. Unfortunately, he'd also had the arrogant and mocking air of a man who was supremely sexy and who knew it. His black eyes had gleamed and suddenly Sorcha had felt unaccountably shy.

'Who…are you?' she questioned.

She rose out of the water like a nymph and Cesare froze, his mouth drying as he saw the firm flesh, green eyes and the lush, perfect curve of her breasts. *Madre di Dio*—but she was exquisite.

'My name is Cesare di Arcangelo,' he murmured, in a velvety-soft accent which matched his exotic looks.

'You're Italian?'

'I am.'

'And… Well…' She didn't want to be rude, but really he could be anyone. And he was so dangerously gorgeous that she felt…*peculiar.* 'What are you doing here?'

'Take a guess, *signorina.*'

'You've come to clean the pool?'

He had never been mistaken for a worker before! Cesare's mouth curved into a smile.

He guessed who *she* must be. Her hair was too wet to see its real colour, but her eyes were green with flecks of gold—a bigger, wider version of her brother's. He knew deep down that there was a long-established rule that you treated your friends' sisters as if they were ice-queens, but it was a rule he found himself suddenly wanting to break.

'Do you want me to?' he drawled. 'Looks pretty clean to me. Anyway, I don't want to interrupt your swim.'

Sorcha shook her wet hair, but something about his hard, lean body was making her pulse race. 'No, that's fine. Don't worry—I've finished now.'

There was a long pause while they stared at one another, and the teasing became something else, while something unknown shimmered on the air.

'So, why don't you get out?'

Did he guess that she was scared to? Because she could feel the tight tingle of desire which was rucking her swimsuit across her breasts and making the tips feel so hard that they hurt?

'I will in a minute.'

'Do you mind if I get in and join you?' He put his hand to the first button on his jeans and shot her a questioning look, but the sight of her dark-eyed confusion made him relent just as Rupert came round the corner.

'Cesare! There you are! Oh, I see you've met Sorcha. Hello, little sister—how are you?'

'Very well,' she said, biting her lip and dipping down into the water in the hope that its coolness might get rid of her embarrassed flush. 'Considering that no one came to meet me at the station.' But she was angry with herself, and with the black-eyed Italian for having made her feel…what?

Desire?

Longing?

She frosted him a look—which wasn't easy on a boiling hot day when your hair was plastered to your head and your heart was racing so much that it felt as if it was going to leap out of your chest. 'Cesare?' she questioned acidly, wondering why the name sounded familiar.

'Cesare di Arcangelo,' he said. 'Rupert and I were at school together.'

'Remember I told you about the Italian who bowled women down like ninepins?' laughed Rupert. 'Owns banks and department stores all over Italy?'

'No,' answered Sorcha in a voice of icy repression. 'I don't believe I do. Rupert, would you mind handing me my towel?'

'Please, allow me.' Cesare had picked up the rather

worn beachtowel and was handing it towards her, holding her gaze with his black eyes. Her coolness intrigued him, for he had never experienced it from a woman before, and her lack of eagerness hinted at a pride and self-possession which was all too rare.

'Forgive me,' he murmured as he held the towel out. 'But I couldn't resist teasing you.' Yet his mockery had been deliberately sensual, and it had been wrong. He had noted her reluctant, embarrassed response—and now he could have kicked himself for subjecting a beautiful young woman to such an onslaught.

He sighed. Her mouth looked as if it were composed of two folded fragrant rose petals which he would have travelled the world to kiss. And he had behaved like some *impacciato* idiot.

And she is the sister of your friend—she is out of bounds.

'*Will* you forgive me?' he persisted.

He sounded as if it mattered, and Sorcha found she couldn't hold out against what seemed to be genuine contrition in his eyes.

'I might,' she said tartly. 'But you'll have to make it up to me.'

He gave a low laugh. 'And how will I go about doing that? Any ideas?' he questioned innocently, and something passed between them at that moment which he had never felt before. The rocket. The thunderbolt. *Colpo di fulmine.* Some random and overwhelming outside force—a kind of unspoken understanding—

which took the universe into the palm of a gigantic hand and began to spin it out of control.

'I'll...I'll think of something,' said Sorcha breathlessly.

'Anything,' he murmured, and at that moment he meant it. 'And it's yours.'

There was an odd kind of silence and then Sorcha hauled herself out of the pool in one fluid movement, water streaming down her long legs. Never had she been so conscious of her body as in the presence of this Italian.

'Cesare's come to cast his expert eye over the Robinsons' latest business plan,' said Rupert. 'I'm hoping I might be able to persuade him to look at ours!'

The Robinsons were their nearest neighbours—fabulously rich, with four eligible sons—one of whom their sister Emma had been dating since *her* schooldays.

'Does that mean I have to be nice to him?' Sorcha asked.

Black eyes now mocked her. 'Very.'

But as she draped the towel over her shoulders Cesare averted his eyes from the body which gleamed like a seal in the tight, wet swimsuit. And wasn't it strange how the smallest courtesy could make you feel safe with a man who was danger personified?

'Do you ride?' she asked suddenly.

Cesare smiled. '*Do* I?'

That was how it started. He'd set off for the Robinsons first thing and return about lunchtime, and Sorcha would be waiting for him in the stables. He would saddle up and they would gallop out together over the lush fields.

And the way her face lit up when she saw him would stab at his heart in a strange and painful way.

'Bet Italy is never as green as this,' she said one afternoon, when they had dismounted and their horses were grazing and she and Cesare were sitting—sweating slightly—beneath the shade of a big oka tree.

'Umbria is very green,' he said.

'Is that where you live?'

'It is where I consider home,' he said, trying and failing not to be rapt by the distracting vision of her breasts thrusting against the fine silk of her riding shirt, her slim legs in jodhpurs and those long, sexy leather boots. He stifled a groan and shifted uncomfortably as she lay on her back, looking up at the leaves.

The air was different today. It felt thick and heavy—as if you could cut through it with a knife—and in the distance was the low murmur of approaching thunder. It reminded him of the storms back home, and the warmth of the soil and the pleasures of the flesh. Cesare could feel a rivulet of sweat trickle down his back, and suddenly he longed to feel her tongue tracing its meandering salty path.

'Really?' she questioned.

He blinked. Really, what? Oh, yes. The weather in Umbria—*just* what he wanted to talk about! 'We have many storms close to Panicale, where I live—but that is why we have such fertile soil.' Fertile. Now, why the hell was he thinking about *that*?

'Have you always lived in Umbria?' Sorcha persisted, because she wanted to know every single thing about him—what he liked for breakfast and what music he listened to, and where was the most beautiful place he'd ever been— 'Umbria, naturally,' he had replied gravely.

'No,' he sighed, 'I grew up in Rome.'

'Tell me,' she whispered.

What was it about women that made them want to tear your soul apart with their questions? And what was it about Sorcha that made him tell her? But he was spare with his facts—a houseful of servants and ever-changing nannies while his parents lived out their jet-set existence. A childhood he did not care to relive in his memory.

And suddenly he could bear it no longer. 'You know that I am having difficulty behaving as a house-guest should behave?' he questioned unsteadily.

Dreamily, Sorcha watched the shimmering canopy of leaves. 'Oh?'

'I want to kiss you.'

She sat up, oblivious to the creamy spill of her cleavage, or the effect it was having on him. On her face was an expression of a tight and bursting excitement— like a child who had just been given a big pile of presents to open.

'Then kiss me. Please.'

He knew in that instant that she was innocent— though he had guessed at it before—and in a way it added to the intolerable weight of his desire, and his position here in the house.

'You know what will happen if I do?' he groaned.

'Yes,' she teased, in an effort to hide her longing, and her nervousness that she would somehow disappoint him—that somehow she wouldn't know what to do. 'Your lips will touch my lips and then— Oh! Oh, *Cesare!*'

'*Si!*' he murmured, as he caught her against him. 'All those things and more. Many more.' He pushed her to the ground and brushed his lips against hers, making a little sound of pleasure in the back of his throat as he coaxed hers into opening.

The kiss went on and on. He had never thought it was possible for a kiss to last so long—he felt he was drowning in it, submerging himself in its sweet potency. The blood pooled and hardened at his groin and he groaned again—only this time the sound was tinged with a sense of urgency.

'Cesare!' she breathed again, as his thumb circled against the tight, damp material which strained over her breast. 'Oh, oh, *oh!*'

He sat up abruptly. This was wrong. Wrong. He sprang to his feet and held out his hand to her. 'Let us move away from here!' he ordered. 'And where in the name of *cielo* is your mother?'

'She's up at the house—why?'

'She is happy for you to ride with me alone every day?' he demanded.

'I think so.'

Did she not know of Cesare di Arcangelo's reputation? he wondered. Did she not realise that women offered themselves to him every day of the week? And would she not be outraged if her daughter were to become just one more in a long line of conquests?

He looked at her, his eyes softening as he saw the bewilderment in hers. For Sorcha was not like the others. She was sweet and innocent.

'Cesare?' Sorcha questioned tentatively.

'It is all right, *cara mia.* Do not frown—for you make lines on that beautiful face.' He kissed the tip of her nose. 'Let's go and swim, and cool off.'

'But Rupert's down by the pool!'

'Exactly,' Cesare said grimly.

But once Cesare kissed Sorcha it was like discovering an addiction which had lain dormant in his body since puberty. It was the first time in his life that he had ever used restraint, but he quickly discovered that sexual frustration was a small price to pay for the slow and erotic discovery of her body. And that delayed sexual gratification was the biggest aphrodisiac in the world.

Sometimes he took pains to make sure that they *weren't* alone together. And he quizzed her on her views so that sometimes Sorcha felt as if he was examining her and ticking off the answers as he went along.

He knew she had a place at university, and he knew that the experience would change her. And—*maledizione!*—was it not human nature for him not to want that?

The long, glorious summer stretched out like an elastic band, and they lived most of it outside. There were parties and dinners and a celebration for Sorcha's exam results, which were even better than predicted, but soon the faint tang of autumn could be felt in the early morning air, and Cesare knew that he could not avoid the real world for ever.

'I have to think about going back,' he said heavily.

She clung to him. 'Why?'

'Because I must. I have stayed longer than I intended.'

'Because of me?' She slanted him a smile, but inside her heart was aching.

'That is one of the reasons,' he agreed evenly, pushing away the memory of the blonde who had told him she was pregnant. It had caused outrage when Cesare had demanded a paternity test, but his certainty that he was not the father had been proven.

He thought how easy it was with Sorcha—and how restful it had been to have a summer free of being hounded by predatory women on the make. He was twenty-six, and he knew that sooner or later he was going to have to settle down—but for the first time in his life he could actually see that it might have some advantages.

He was confused.

He wanted her, and yet to take her virginity would be too huge a responsibility, would abuse his position as guest.

He wanted her, but still he hesitated—because he wanted to savour the near-torture of abstinence, recognising that the wait had been so long and so exquisitely painful that nothing would ever feel this acute again.

He wanted her, and yet in his heart he knew that he could have her only at a huge price.

'Oh, Sorcha,' he groaned, and knew that he could not go on like this. *'Siete cosi donna bella.'*

He pulled her into his arms and began to kiss her, softly at first, and then seekingly—so that her lips opened like a shell, with her tongue the wet, precious pearl within.

With a savage groan he cupped her breast, feeling its lush, pert weight resting in the palm of his hand. He flicked his thumb against the hardening nipple and knew that with much more of this he would suckle her in full daylight. And what else?

'We can't stay here,' he said grimly.

'Let's go inside,' she begged.

He had held out for so long, until he was stretched to breaking point, and silently he took her hand and led her into the house, to the darkened study, whose windows were shuttered against the blinding sunlight.

They kissed frantically—hard and desperately—and suddenly Cesare's hands were all over her in a way he'd never allowed them to be before. He pushed her down onto a leather couch. His hand was rucking up her dress, feeling her thighs part, and as he inched his thumb upwards she writhed in silent invitation.

He had just scraped aside her damp panties and pushed a finger into her sweet, sticky warmth when they heard the sound of a door slamming at the far end of the house. Sorcha sat bolt upright and stared at him with wide, frightened eyes. He pulled his hand away from her.

'*Merda!*' he swore softly. 'Who is it?'

'It must be my mother!'

'Are you sure?'

'Who else could it be?'

Hurriedly he smoothed his hands down over her ruffled hair and silently left the room, disappearing for the rest of the afternoon until just before pre-dinner drinks were served when he went to find her alone, sitting on the terrace, her face unhappy.

He knew that the timing was wrong—but he also knew that this must be said now. He felt as you sometimes did when you walked through the sticky mud of a ploughed field after a rainstorm. It was the price he knew must be paid for his body's desire, and yet he was too het up to question whether it was too high.

'Sorcha, will you be my wife?'

She stared at him. '*What did you say?*' she whispered.

'Will you marry me?'

Rocked and reeling with pure astonishment that such a question should have come out of the blue, Sorcha heard only the reluctance in his voice, and saw the strained expression on his face.

'Why?' She fed him the question like a stage stooge setting up the punchline, but he failed to deliver it.

'Need you ask? You are accomplished and very beautiful, and you are intelligent and make me laugh. And as well as your many obvious attributes you are a virgin, and that is a rare prize in the world in which we live.'

'A *rare prize?*' she joked. 'That matters to you?'

'Of course it matters to me!' His black eyes narrowed and his macho heritage came to the fore. 'I want to possess you totally, utterly, Sorcha—in a way that no other man ever has nor ever will. And I think we have what it takes to make a successful marriage.'

He was talking about her as if she was something he could own or take over—like swallowing up a smaller company.

And it was the most damning answer he could have given. Sorcha was not yet nineteen and she hadn't even begun to live. She was at an age where love was far more important than talking cold-bloodedly about a marriage's chance of success. Yes, she had fallen in love with Cesare—but he had said nothing about loving her back. And how could she possibly marry him and give the rest of her life to him in those circumstances? And throw her hard-fought-for university education away into the bargain.

He would get over it—and so would she. Yes, it would hurt—but just imagine the pain of an inevitable failed marriage with a man who didn't love her? That damning phrase came back to echo round in her head.

A rare prize.

She looked at him, masking her terrible hurt with an expression of pride.

'No, Cesare,' she said quietly. 'I can't marry you.'

CHAPTER THREE

THE bridesmaids' limousine pulled up in front of Whittaker House, and Sorcha helped the little ones clamber down, forcing herself to concentrate on the present in the hope that it might take her mind away from that last painful night with Cesare and its aftermath.

She remembered the way he had looked at her after she had turned down his proposal of marriage—with bitterness in his brilliant black eyes. She had tried to explain that she wanted to do her university course and get some kind of career under her belt, and that had seemed to make him angrier still.

And she would never forget the things he had said to her. The things he had accused her of. That she was a tease and that some men would not have acted with his restraint—and that he should have taken her when she had offered herself to him so freely.

How could deep affection so quickly have been transmuted into something so dark and angry?

That day they had crossed the line from almost-lovers into a place where there could never be anything but mutual distrust and hatred on his part.

And on hers?

Well, she had vowed to forget him, and to a certain extent she had succeeded—but her recovery had been by no means total. For her, seeing him today was like someone who suffered from a dreadful craving being given a hit of their particular drug. And even though she could see contempt in his eyes, hear the silken scorn in his voice, that wasn't enough to eradicate the hunger she still felt for him.

But she could not afford the self-indulgence of allowing herself to wallow in the past because it was the present that mattered. And it was only a day—when she had an important role to fulfil and surely the necessary strength of character to withstand the presence here of the man she had once loved.

Pinning a smile to her mouth, she swallowed down the dryness in her throat and looked around the grounds.

There was certainly a lot to take in. The gravel had been raked, the lawn had been mowed into perfect emerald stripes, and not a single weed peeped from any of the flowerbeds. She had never seen her home look so magnificent, but then for once cash had been no object.

Emma had been going out with Ralph Robinson since for ever, and her new husband was sweet and charming—but most of all he was rich. In fact, he was rolling in money, and he had splashed lots of it about in an effort to ensure that he and Emma had the kind of wedding which would be talked about in years to come. And Whittaker House might be crumbling at the seams, but no one could deny it looked good in photographs.

The youngest of the bridesmaids tugged Sorcha's dress.

'Can I have ice-cream, please, Sorcha?' she pleaded. 'Mummy said if I was a good girl in church I could have ice-cream.'

'And you shall—but you must eat your dinner up first,' said Sorcha. 'Just stay with me until we're in the marquee, so we don't get lost—because we're all sitting at a big, special table with the bride and groom.'

'Bride and *gloom*, Daddy always says,' offered the more precocious of the pageboys.

'Very funny, Alex,' said Sorcha, but the smile on her face died as she saw Cesare climbing out of a low silver sports car, then opening the door for the brunette.

Sorcha stared at her in disgust—the woman's dress had ridden so far up her thighs that, as she swung her legs out of the car—she was practically showing her underwear. Didn't she know that there were graceful ways to get out of a car without showing the world what you'd had for breakfast?

And why should you care?

But if she didn't care—which she didn't—then why did Sorcha find it impossible to tear her eyes away from him? Because Cesare could have been hers, and now she would never know what it would have been like—was that it? Somehow it didn't matter how many times you told yourself that you had made the right choice—you couldn't stop the occasional regret. And regret was a terrible emotion to live with.

The brunette was laughing up at him, her fleshy lips gleaming provocatively—with sensual promise written on every atom of her being.

'Come along, children,' Sorcha said quickly, before he caught her studying him like some sort of crazed stalker.

But Cesare saw Sorcha bend and tie a bow in a little cherub's curls and giggle at something the little one said and his mouth twisted. He knew that women sometimes used children as a prop when men were watching them—a silent demonstration of what wonderful mothers they would eventually make. Was that pretty little tableau all for *his* benefit, he thought sourly, to show him what he'd missed? Oh, but he was going to enjoy her reaction when she discovered what was coming to her! Abruptly, he turned away to toss his car keys to a valet.

Sorcha led the clutch of children around to the marquee, feeling a bit like the Pied Piper of Hamelin, but the presence of Cesare was like a dark spectre lurking in the background.

How the hell was she going to react to him for the rest of the afternoon and evening, if the mere sight of him unsettled her enough to set her pulse racing and set off all kinds of feelings churning around inside her?

She walked into the marquee, which looked as if it was competing for inclusion in the Chelsea Flower

Show, and for a moment her dark mood evaporated. She forgot all about Cesare and all worries about the business and just enjoyed the spectacle of her sister's wedding reception instead.

There were blooms everywhere—tumbling and filling and falling over in tall urns dotted around the sides of the tented room—and ivy wreathed around the pillars. Roses were crammed into copper pots on each table, reflected back in the gleaming crystal and golden cutlery, so that the whole room looked a mass of glorious, vibrant colour.

Maybe they could hire the house out as a wedding venue on a professional basis? she found herself thinking. Wouldn't that help the current cashflow situation?

She reunited her young charges with their parents until the meal began, showed an elderly aunt to her seat, and then dashed to the loo to reapply her lipstick. But when eventually she couldn't put it off any longer, she began to walk towards the top table—and her heart sank with a dull dread when she saw who was dominating it, perfectly at ease, with the lazy kind of grace which seemed to come to him as naturally as breathing.

She could see her mother at the far end in her huge hat, shrugging her shoulders in a *don't-ask-me* kind of way. But even more annoying was that Cesare appeared to have captured the attention of the entire room—and it was supposed to be the bride's day!

His ruggedly handsome and impeccably dressed figure was exciting jealous glances from men as well as greedy ones from women, and as she grew closer Sorcha could hear people on the adjoining tables.

'Who is he?'

'A rich Italian, apparently!'

'Available?

'Let's hope so!'

But Cesare wasn't reacting to the interest buzzing around him—his black eyes were trained on only her, so that by the time she reached him Sorcha felt as jittery as if she had just walked the plank and was about to jump.

She stared at the thick black hair which once she had had the freedom to run her hands through, and those slanting, aristocratic cheekbones along which she had wonderingly traced a trembling fingertip as if unable to believe that he was real and in her arms. 'You,' she said, and was appalled to hear her voice tremble.

'Me,' he agreed, his eyes glittering with satisfaction as he saw the look of consternation on her face.

She gripped the back of her seat. 'Is this some kind of bad joke?'

'If it is then I must have missed the punchline,' he answered silkily. 'Am I making you feel weak at the knees, *cara?* You seem a little unsteady on your feet. Why don't you sit down?'

He pulled the chair out for her and she sank into it, too shaky to defy his commanding manner and wondering if she had imagined the feather-light touch of his hand across her bare shoulder. 'How have you managed to get yourself seated on the top table? And next to *me?* Did you change the *placement?*' she questioned suspiciously.

He thought how she had grown in confidence over the ensuing years, how the shy young girl had gone for ever, and his blood heated. Oh, yes, this time he would enjoy her without compunction.

'No, I did not change the *placement,*' he said softly. 'Perhaps they felt sorry for you, being on your own. I take it you *are* on your own, Sorcha?'

Oh, how she wished that she had managed to sustain some of those random dates she'd had into something approaching a proper relationship. How she would have loved to rub Cesare di Arcangelo's smug and arrogant face in it if she could have airily produced some unbelievably gorgeous and eligible hunk and said, in that way that women did, I'm-not-trying-to-be-smug-or-anything-but-this-is-my-*boyfriend!*

But how could she have done, even if such a figure had really existed? Whoever she lined up—however rich and however eligible—would fade into humdrum insignificance beside the luminous sex appeal of Cesare.

'Yes, I am on my own,' she said coolly, because she had learnt that being defensive about it only made people probe even more. 'I don't need a man to define me.'

'Well, that's lucky, isn't it?' he mocked.

'Why are you bothering to sit next to me if all you want to do is insult me?' she hissed.

'Oh, but that isn't *all* I want to do, *cara mia.*' The black eyes roamed over her with breathtaking arrogance, lingering on the lush swell of her breasts, and very deliberately he ran the tip of his tongue around the inside of his mouth. 'There are plenty of other things I'd like to do to you which are far more appealing.'

Sorcha turned her head, desperately hoping that someone might come to her rescue, swoop down on her and whisk her away from him. But no one came, and no one was likely to interrupt them—since the *don't disturb us* vibes which were shimmering off Cesare's powerful frame were almost tangible.

Maybe they needed to have this conversation. She hadn't seen him since that day when he'd packed his bags and managed—she'd never been quite sure how— to get a helicopter with a stunning woman pilot to land on the front lawn and whisk him away.

And after today she wasn't likely to see him again. So maybe this really would help her to move on—to eliminate his legacy of being the man whom no other could possibly live up to. Maybe she needed to accept that by settling for someone who didn't have his dynamism and sex appeal she would actually be happier in the long run.

'Just say whatever it is you want to say, Cesare.'

It occurred to him that she might be shocked if he gave her a graphic rundown of just what he would like to be doing to her right then, and he ran one long olive finger around the rim of his wine glass.

'What are you doing these days?' he questioned.

Sorcha blinked at him suspiciously, like a person

emerging from the darkness into light. 'You want to hear about my life?' she asked warily.

He smiled up at the waitress who was heaping smoked salmon onto his plate and shrugged. 'We have two choices, Sorcha,' he said softly. 'We can talk about the past and our unfulfilled sexual history, which might make us a little…how is it that you say…? Ah, yes. Hot under the collar.' His gaze drifted to her bare neck. 'Not that you're wearing a collar, of course,' he murmured. 'And it would be a pity to taint that magnificent chest with unsightly blotches, don't you think?'

Sorcha lifted her hands to her cheeks as they began to burn. 'Stop it,' she begged, and cursed the debilitating effect of desire which had turned her voice into a whisper.

'You see? It's happening already. And it's all your fault for being so damned sexy,' he chided, but he realised he had made himself a victim of his own teasing, and that his erection was pushing hard against his thigh. He shifted uncomfortably. Only this time the brakes were off. She wasn't eighteen any more, but a woman—and he was no longer morally obliged to handle her with kid gloves.

'The alternative is that we make polite conversation like every other guest in the room. Safer by far, don't you think?'

Sorcha swallowed as she felt the blood-rush slowly drain from her face. Safer? Today he looked about as safe as a killer shark! Had she been blind to his almost tangible sex appeal before—or just naïve enough to think that he would protect her from it?

And he had, hadn't he? He had treated her like a piece of delicate porcelain.

Sorcha bit her lip—because what was the point in remembering that? She didn't want to feel soft and warm about him—not when his eyes were gleaming dark and intimidating fire at her. But she wasn't going to let him intimidate her, was she? All she had to do was get through this ordeal without showing any further sign of weakness, then it would be over and Cesare would be gone—and with him all the bittersweet memories he evoked.

She watched the bubbles in her champagne glass fizzing their way to the surface. 'So what do you want to know?'

'Where are you living these days?'

'I'm…' She hesitated. *At home* made her sound as if she were five years old. 'Living at the house.'

'Really? Isn't that a little—' he shrugged his shoulders '—repressive?'

Now, why did she feel stung into defence? 'It's an enormous house—and anyway, I've only just moved back. I've been living and working in London. I've bought a flat up there, actually—but I'm renting it out at the moment.'

'Really?' he mocked, and his mouth hardened. 'And what about your *career*?'

There was something in his tone which she didn't like or recognise. Almost as if he were going through the mechanics of asking her questions to which he already knew the answers. Or was she just being paranoid, crediting him with powers he didn't have simply because his attempts at 'conversation' sounded like an interrogation?

But she was proud of her work—and why shouldn't he damned well know it? 'I got a job straight after university for one of the best firms in the city and I worked for them until recently. They offered me promotion to stay, but I...' What was it about his manner which made her reluctant to tell him? 'I decided to work for the family firm instead. So here I am.'

He raised his dark brows. 'Ah! That explains it.'

'Explains what?' Sorcha frowned. 'I don't have a clue what you're talking about.'

'You don't? Forgive me, *cara*—I should have said nothing.' He lifted the palms of his hands upwards in an apologetic gesture, although his face didn't look in the least bit apologetic.

'No,' said Sorcha coldly. 'You can't dangle a carrot like that and then snatch it away.'

'I can do any damned thing I please,' he retorted. 'But I will take pity on you.' He shrugged his broad shoulders, enjoying seeing the convulsive little swallow in her long throat at his deliberate use of the word *pity*. 'It's just that rumours in the business world...well, you know what they can be like.'

'I never listen to rumours,' she said fiercely. 'Whittakers has had a few problems, it's true—but we're undergoing an upturn and things are looking good!'

'*Good?*' Cesare smiled, but it was a hard smile

edged with scorn. 'What a hopeless little liar you are,' he said softly. 'Whittakers is going down the pan fast—and if you don't know that then you aren't fit to be employed by them.'

If she had been anywhere else but sitting at the top table at her sister's wedding, wearing enough aquamarine silk-satin to curtain the entire staterooms of a large cruise-liner, then Sorcha would have stood up and left the table. But apart from the obvious logistics of rapid movement in such a voluminous garment—she had a duty to fulfil. She knew that, and he knew it, too.

'Every company goes through a rough patch from time to time,' she defended.

'Some do. It's just that Whittakers seems to be enjoying a permanent rough patch,' he drawled.

And suddenly Sorcha wondered why on earth she was tolerating this egotistical man giving her the benefit of his opinion. She hadn't asked for it, and she didn't particularly want it.

She glanced across the room as if he hadn't spoken, to where the brunette was sitting with an untouched plate of food and an empty wine glass, staring at him like a hungry dog.

Sorcha gave him a cool smile. 'Did you really come here today to discuss the fortunes of Whittakers?' she questioned lightly. 'I'm sure you could find more interesting things to do than snipe on about profit and loss!'

He followed the direction of her gaze and smiled.

'I'm sure I could,' he murmured. 'But I'm not looking for a one-night-stand—at least not tonight, and not with her. I'm going to enjoy getting to know my new colleagues instead.'

There was triumph gleaming from his black eyes, and the smile of pure elation which curved his mouth sent Sorcha's pulse skittering. But this time it was not desire which was making her feel almost dizzy, but fear—a nebulous, unformed fear which was solidifying by the minute.

'Colleagues? What colleagues?'

He savoured the moment, knowing that in years to come he'd remember this as the moment when his obsession with her had finally lifted.

'You and I are going to be working together,' he murmured.

'What are you talking about?'

'Rupert has brought me into the company as trouble-shooter.'

The chatter of the guests receded and then came roaring back again, so loud that Sorcha wanted to clamp her hands over her ears and stare at Cesare in disbelief.

'I don't believe you. He wouldn't do that.' Her shocked words sounded as though she was speaking under water.

He shrugged his broad shoulders. 'Why wouldn't he?'

'Because…because…' *Because he knows the history between us.* But that was the trouble. Rupert didn't. No one did. Not really. They had kept it pretty much hidden, and afterwards she certainly hadn't confided that there had been a proposal of marriage. She suspected that they would have looked at her as if she was crazy to turn a man like Cesare down.

So she had locked it away, thinking that the less said, the sooner it would be mended. And in theory it should have worked. A summer squall of a love affair should have just blown over—but Cesare's legacy had been to leave an unerasable memory of him stubbornly lurking in her mind.

'Rupert wouldn't have done something like that without asking me first.'

'Are you sure, *cara*?' he questioned cynically. 'I suggest you ask your brother.'

Sorcha's throat dried, because there was something in his eyes which told her that he was telling the truth. And she knew then that her instincts had been right after all. He hadn't just shown up at the wedding to join in the celebrations, hand over an exquisite present and say hi to all his adoring fans. 'No,' she whispered.

'Yes,' he said grimly.

'But why?'

'Is that a serious question?' he demanded. 'Surely you must know that if something is not done soon, then Whittakers will cease to exist.'

Sorcha shook her head. 'That's not what I mean, and you know it. I don't believe you're operating out of the goodness of your heart. This can't just be because you've seen an ailing company and you want to increase its profitability.'

'Why else could it be?'

'Because…' She thought of the way he'd been looking at her, the things he'd been saying to her, the sense of something dark and sensual and unfinished between them. 'Because I think you want to sleep with me.'

He laughed softly. 'Oh, Sorcha,' he murmured. 'Of course I do. And how refreshing of you to acknowledge it so early on. I've heard of performance-related bonuses, but this puts a whole new slant on the subject!' He started laughing. 'Tell me, *cara*—are you offering me what in business terms is known as a *golden hello*?'

Her fingers were itching. She would have liked to rake them down his rugged olive cheek or to curl them around a glass of sticky liqueur and hurl it all over his pristine white shirt.

He glanced down at them. 'Don't even think of it,' he warned quietly. 'We don't want a scene at your sister's wedding, do we? Or do you want to grapple with me in order to get me to kiss you?'

He rose to his feet and looked down at her with eyes which had suddenly grown hard as jet, and Sorcha stared at him, realising that beneath all the civilised veneer there was nothing but coldness in his face.

'You're going?' she questioned, her heart pounding painfully in her chest.

'I'm expecting a call.'

'Don't you know it isn't done to just disappear from a wedding breakfast before the toasts?'

'Thanks for the etiquette lesson,' he said softly. 'But

I've squared it with Rupert. Just make sure you're in the office tomorrow morning first thing. Eight o'clock. I like to start early, so don't be late.'

Sorcha wanted to say something cutting and brilliant—to tell him that he had no right to order her around as if she was his subordinate. But he was right—they didn't want a scene at her sister's wedding. She was forced to endure the sight of him leaving, while the brunette in yellow made an unseemly scramble to her feet and followed him out of the marquee.

CHAPTER FOUR

'WHAT do you mean you *had no alternative*?' demanded Sorcha, raking her fingers distractedly through her hair, which was already rumpled.

She turned to face Rupert, the morning sun bright on his face as it flooded into the boardroom which was lined with framed posters advertising the famous Whittaker Sauce. Each one featured an apple-cheeked old lady stirring a steaming pot, a look of satisfaction on her face, and the splash line was: JUST LIKE GRANDMA USED TO MAKE!

Sorcha's green eyes sparked accusatory fire at her brother, but inside she was hurting. 'You mean that someone was holding a gun to your head and telling you that you had no alternative but to hire Cesare di Arcangelo to save the company?'

'No, of course not—'

'Well, *why*, then?'

'You've seen for yourself how bad things are, Sorcha. And Cesare has a reputation for turning things around—

look what he did for the Robinsons. Their profits went through the stratosphere! I gave him a call, not really thinking that he'd have the time available, and when he offered to come over straight away I couldn't believe it.'

'Couldn't you?' Sorcha shook her head. How naïve Rupert sounded—but then he just saw Cesare for what he thought he was, without understanding the complexity of the man's nature or the deviousness of his mind. 'But *I'm* here, now, Rupes. I came back here specially, to be Marketing Director. Shouldn't you at least have discussed it with me first?'

There was a silence.

'But, Sorcha, you've only just started with the company,' said Rupert gently. 'What with the wedding and all—I simply haven't had the chance to tell you before now, that's all. And there's nothing really *to* discuss, is there? You know that Cesare's reputation is legendary. So who in their right mind would throw up an opportunity to have him work for them?'

Who indeed? Women who'd had their hearts broken didn't count—or rather, their feelings weren't up for consideration in the big, brash world of finance.

She had been caught on the back foot—feeling not only cheated but shocked by her near-lover's reappearance. But even if she'd *known* that Cesare was about to dramatically reappear in her life would it have actually changed anything, other than allowing her time to prepare her response to him?

And would that response have been any different?

Could it have been? Even if she had been the greatest actress in the world and pinned the brightest smile to her lips that wouldn't have changed the uncomfortable cocktail of emotions he had stirred up, would it?

Rupert sighed. 'I'm sorry, Sorcha—but, whatever your private opinion of Cesare, nobody can deny the man's reputation as a sharpshooter.'

'Don't you mean an egotistical control freak who can't keep it in his trousers?' she questioned bitterly.

'Rule one of business,' drawled a velvety voice from behind her, and Sorcha whirled round to see Cesare walking into the room, a briefcase under his arm and a glint in his black eyes. 'Never badmouth your colleagues within earshot. Didn't they teach you that at business school, Sorcha?' He put the briefcase down on the vast desk. 'What else is it that you English say? Walls have ears? *Ciao,* Rupert.'

Sorcha wanted to scream—feeling as if she'd just been given a walk-on part in someone else's life. That this couldn't really be happening. There was nowhere to look but at Cesare, but even if there had been she wondered if she'd be able to keep her eyes off him.

He was dressed to look as if he meant business, which meant a suit—but something in the way he wore it transformed it from the mere everyday garment which other men wore to work.

It looked cool enough to be linen and fine enough to be silk, exquisitely cut in the Italian style—loose-fitting and utterly modern, yet hinting at the pure, hard muscle beneath. She found herself searching his face for dark shadows, wondering if he had gone home with the brunette last night, and it bothered her that she should even think about it—that it could make her heart contract with jealousy.

'You underhand swine!' she accused.

'Sorcha!' choked her brother.

There wasn't a flicker of reaction on Cesare's face. 'Rupert—would you mind going on ahead to the factory?' he said evenly. 'I'll join you just as soon as I can.'

'Sure thing,' said Rupert, who seemed glad of the escape route.

'Oh, and Rupert?'

'Mmm?'

'I may be a little time,' Cesare murmured, his black eyes fixed unwavering on Sorcha.

'Yeah.'

There was a pin-drop silence while Rupert left the room and closed the door behind him, and Cesare put his hands on his narrow hips and looked at her.

Way back he had vetoed mixing business with pleasure, and he wouldn't usually have been turned on by a woman wearing severely cut office clothes, but in Sorcha's case it was different. He felt a nerve flicker in his cheek.

Two top buttons of her plain silk shirt were unbuttoned, showing a sliver of a gold chain with a pearl attached which dipped invitingly towards the shadow of her cleavage. A classic pencil skirt clung to the pert line of her bottom and skated down over her thighs. Cesare wondered how he could have forgotten the slender curve of her hips, or how long and rangy her legs were—especially in those high heels.

She was like a very classy racehorse—all athletic power and stamina sheathed by sheer elegance. A woman in peak and very beautiful condition. Why the hell hadn't he just had her when he'd had the opportunity, guaranteeing her nothing but a postscript in the catalogue of his sexual experience?

'I think that you and I need to have a little talk, don't you, *cara*?' he questioned silkily.

Sorcha's heart was pounding. Yesterday at the wedding, when he had told her that he had been brought in, it had been nothing more than a theoretical nightmare. Today, however, it was harsh reality, with him standing beside the shiny table her father had used to sit at as if he were born to stand there—arrogantly wielding all the power. But she was *not* going to let him intimidate her.

'You've come up with a magic solution to all our problems, have you, Cesare?'

'*Soluzione magica?*' he mocked. 'Aren't you a little old to believe in fairytales? No. But I have a few ideas.'

I'll bet you do. Sorcha stared at him stonily as he pulled out a sheaf of papers from his briefcase and flicked through them until he found the ones he was looking for. Then he leaned forward and spread them out on the table like a card-dealer, looking up at her with a question in his glittering ebony eyes. 'You have studied all these figures which highlight the company's decline with heartbreaking accuracy?'

'Of course I have.'

'Really?' His eyes burned into her, his lips curving around his cold, judgemental words. 'And what course of action do you propose we take to halt the downturn?'

He was enjoying this, Sorcha realised furiously. In the same way that a policeman might enjoy interrogating a guilty suspect or a sadist might enjoy pulling the wings off a butterfly. And he would enjoy it even more if she allowed him to see that he was getting to her. So she wouldn't.

It was easier said than done. She moved her shoulders edgily. 'I'm looking into sales movements, distribution patterns, rises and falls in trading—you know. The usual thing.'

'Yes. Precisely. Hashing over the past. *The usual thing,*' he agreed, leaping on her phrase and repeating it with icy sarcasm. 'But innovation is everything in business—you must know that, Sorcha. Working for the family firm doesn't mean you have to undergo a common sense bypass.'

'You think you're very clever, don't you, Cesare?'

'I think that's a given,' he retorted softly. 'But this has nothing to do with ego or brains, and everything to do with achievement!'

His eyes were blazing now, and even though he was revelling in the mutinous expression on her lovely face it was by no means what motivated him. Because—no matter what unfinished business there was between him and Sorcha Whittaker—this was all about pride, and a very different kind of pride from the one she had wounded by her refusal to marry him.

He had taken on this task and it was a challenge—and Cesare was a man who always rose to a challenge and conquered it.

The Whittaker scheme interested him only in the way in which an overfed cat might be mildly interested in a small mouse which had foolishly strayed into its path. But the venture afforded him the delicious opportunity to seduce the only woman he'd ever asked to marry. Turning around the ailing company was a purely secondary consideration, and he knew that he could easily afford to fail. In fact, lesser men might have got some perverse kind of pleasure from seeing her made broke.

But even if he hadn't been loyal to Rupert, Cesare's nature and his need to succeed were such that he would not tolerate failure—of any kind—and didn't his relationship with Sorcha represent just that? Surely the ultimate satisfaction would be to bed her, win the praise of her family by reviving their fortunes, and make a packet for himself into the bargain? Put her for ever in his debt before walking away—this time for good, giving her the rest of her life to reflect on what she could have had. Yes. A perfect plan.

Prendere due piccioni con una fava.

To kill two birds with one stone…

He sighed. *Si.*

His raised his eyes, enjoying the frustration which she was failing to hide. 'Rupert has been trying to drum up more trade—but you've got a brain in your head, Sorcha. Didn't it occur to you to put it to use to try and work out why the products aren't selling?'

'You think it's that easy?'

He shook his dark head. 'Not easy, no. Simple, yes. Sit down.'

She hesitated, and then perched on the edge of the boardroom table instead of pulling out one of the chairs which stood around it. His eyes mocked her.

'Demonstrating your equality?' he murmured.

'You wouldn't know equality if it reached out and bit you!'

Laughing softly, he sat down in one of the soft leather chairs and leaned back to look at her, wondering if she would have chosen such a highly visible vantage point if she had realised the view it gave him of her derrière. Or that the material of her skirt was stretched so tightly over her bottom that he could see the faint outline of a thong.

His resulting erection made him wince. *Serves you right,* he thought, as he reached down into his briefcase. 'I've been going back through the Whittakers advertising budget over the past year—'

'It would be madness to cut the budget,' she interjected quickly.

'I'm not suggesting we do—please don't put words in my mouth,' he snapped. *Put your breast in my mouth instead.* His erection grew even harder as he pulled out a copy of a popular women's magazine. 'Take a look at this.'

She did as he asked, glad to have the opportunity to look away from that hard and fascinating face and concentrate on something other than the soft, warm coil of desire which was slowly unfurling in the pit of her stomach.

Why couldn't she just be impartial to him—good looks or no good looks? She'd met men who were almost as hunky as Cesare—though it was true that they didn't seem to have his inbuilt arrogance, or the ability to be in charge of a situation wherever he happened to be at the time.

She didn't want to *feel* anything other than maybe a vaguely grown-up sensation of *There's the man I thought I was in love with—the man who asked me to marry him.* She wanted to feel that thing you were supposed to feel when you looked at someone from a past which seemed very dim and distant—that she was looking at a complete stranger. So why didn't she?

Trying to quell the tremble in her fingers, she flicked through the magazine he had given her. There was a big spread on a former weathergirl's latest attempt to conquer her weight problem, with a few tantalising insights as to why she was attracted to violent men, there were gossip items and recipes, a problem page and a fashion shoot, and—amongst the other advertise-ments—an ad for Whittakers.

Sorcha had grown up seeing bottles of the family sauce plastered over various publications since the year dot, so it was no big deal—but she always felt a little glow of satisfaction when she saw one of their full-colour promotions.

'You mean this?' She looked up at him. 'It's good, isn't it?'

'It's good for what it is,' he answered carefully.

'Why are you talking in riddles, Cesare—am I supposed to be looking for anything in particular?'

He studied her lips and thought how he would like to wipe that nonchalant expression off her beautiful face with a long, hard kiss. 'Does anything about it strike you as different?'

'Not really.'

'*Not really,*' he echoed, biting back his irritation. He leaned back further in his chair. 'It's the same advert you've been using for years.'

'So what? It's a good advert!'

'I will tell you *so what, cara,*' he said softly. 'If companies do not change—then they die—that is a rule of life which applies to everything and everyone. And it shows a certain arrogance towards the general public if you treat them with contempt, not even wanting to bother to *try* and change.'

She stiffened. '*You* have the nerve to talk about arrogance?'

Cesare drew in a deep breath. He would have liked nothing better than to talk about arrogance, since it was the kind of subject which soon had women railing and then pouting and then sending out messages which would result in a silent little tussle, and then… then… But he couldn't risk making love to her. Not yet.

'We are going to be changing the campaign.'

'Shouldn't that be a question rather than a state-ment? Or have you been given *carte blanche* to do exactly what you want without running it past me first?' she demanded.

He didn't bother answering that, and the fact that she didn't pick up on it meant that she was perceptive enough to realise that maybe she wouldn't like the answer. 'Granny cooking up home recipes on the kitchen table no longer strikes a chord,' he said slowly.

'But people relate to that! They think it really *is* great-granny! The whole family business thing is what defines us! It's what makes us different to all the other brands!'

'I know that.' He paused. 'And that is why we're planning to upgrade the company with a brand-new image—spearheaded by one of its very own family members. A new generation to front the Whittaker campaign. Imagine the publicity.'

'And just which member of the family did you have in mind to front this new advertising campaign?' The question sounded mechanical, because even as she was asking it she knew that there was just her, her mother and Rupert. Unless Cesare meant *Emma,* and she was away on her honeymoon.

He gave the ghost of a smile. 'Oh, come on, Sorcha,' he said softly. 'You may not have impressed me with your business acumen so far, but there is only one person who can do it. You know that and I know that.' His black eyes glittered. 'And that person is you, *bella donna.*'

CHAPTER FIVE

SORCHA froze as she looked into Cesare's dark, mocking face. 'No.'

'No?' he echoed.

She clenched her fists. 'If you want someone to front your new advertising campaign, you'll have to look somewhere else.'

'But we've already decided that it has to be a family member—your mother is the wrong age, your sister is the wrong marital status, and your brother is the wrong sex.' His lips curved into a smile. 'We want to reach out and capture the single person who is living on their own—to introduce a whole new market to a very traditional product.'

'No, Cesare.'

'Why not?'

'Because I'm not a model!'

'Ah, but that is the whole point—we don't want a professional model,' he murmured silkily, and he bent down to pick up a large black cardboard envelope from which he pulled a thick sheet of cartridge paper in the manner of a magician withdrawing a rabbit from a hat. He handed it to her.

Inside was a mock-up of an advertisement featuring a girl with bright strawberry blonde hair—drawn to look just like her, she realised with a sinking feeling. On the table in front of her were all the delicious ingredients of a sandwich in the making, with a bottle of Whittakers Hot n' Spicy in the foreground.

The girl was sucking her finger, her eyes gazing wide and coquettish at the camera, and just one word was splashed across the top of the page. SAUCY!

'Simple, but effective,' said Cesare, and he felt weak with desire just imagining Sorcha sucking on *his* finger, and on…

'Just imagine the publicity,' he said huskily. 'This could be big, Sorcha. Really big.'

'And if demand increases—just how are you planning to meet it? Are you just going to magic up X amount of sauce from nowhere, Cesare?'

He gave her a narrow-eyed look of admiration. 'Leave that to me.'

He spoke in a tone of voice which told her that nothing was going to be a problem—and, infuriatingly, she believed him. But he hadn't taken into account the unpredictability of human nature had he? Or of women in particular? 'You've thought of everything, haven't you?' she breathed.

His smile was satisfied as he waited for the plaudits to come his way. 'I've tried,' he murmured.

'Well, you should have consulted *me,* shouldn't you?' she questioned crisply. 'Because I can't do this.'

His smile vanished. 'Why not?'

'The rest of the family would never agree to me taking centre-stage.'

'They already have.'

They already have.

'Emma thinks it would be good for you.'

Emma thinks it would be good for you.

'And your mother—'

'Stop it!' she screeched. 'I don't want to hear!'

It had taken a moment or two for her to register what had been niggling at her all along, but his words helped it to snap into crystal-clear focus.

Not only had he been brought in behind her back and then demanded that she be kept in the dark until it was too late to do anything to change it. But now—just as if they were engaged in some old-fashioned spy story— he had been briefing against her. It appeared that he had been masterminding a whole great scheme involving her—only she was the last person to know!

Sorcha glanced at the beautifully executed mock-up. This wasn't something which he had just had an artist scribble up in a few minutes—this had all been carefully planned. She had been excluded, and the rest of the family had colluded with him. It felt like a betrayal in the most complete sense of the word.

'You must have been working behind my back for weeks,' she said in a stunned voice.

'I thought it preferable if we presented it to you as a *fait accompli.*'

She looked at him, stunned. 'You bastard,' she said softly.

Cesare's blood heated with an inevitable sense of triumph—because, in a way, wasn't this exactly what he had wanted all along? For the precarious veneer of civility which had existed between them to be smashed by a simple word of contempt—leaving him free to give in to what he had wanted to do from the moment he'd first laid eyes on her again. And everyone knew that conflict made the best aphrodisiac in the world.

'Is that what I am?' he questioned as he walked towards her. Her eyes were filled with fury—and something else, too—or were they just mirroring what was in his? An unbearable hunger he had only just realised had been building away inside him all these years.

'Then maybe I'd better start behaving like one.' And with one unequivocal gesture he pulled her to her feet and into his arms.

She saw it coming—of course she did—but the pressure of his arms and the heat of his body drove everything from her mind—other than how much she had dreamed about this over the years, despite all her best efforts to suppress it. Sometimes in the middle of the cruel and indiscriminate night she had awoken to relive the achingly unfulfilled pleasure of his kiss—as someone stranded in the desert might remember how a glass of cool water tasted.

'Bastard!' she said again, but it came out on a shuddering breath of pleasure as he splayed his fingers possessively over her back. And this time something had changed. She was no longer eighteen years old, with a watchful mother lurking around in the house and a man who almost didn't trust himself to touch her for fear that he would lose control. He was certainly trusting himself to touch her now.

She felt her knees weakening, so that instead of wrenching herself away from him she sank inexorably against him. It felt as if every taut muscle and sinew was imprinted against her. A body like rock and skin like silk—when had she learned to find that particular combination so utterly irresistible?

'Damn you,' she managed indistinctly. 'Oh, damn you, Cesare di Arcangelo!'

'But you don't want to damn me,' he taunted.

'Yes, I do,' she returned, and wondered how her voice could sound so reedy.

His gaze raked over her face and read the stark hunger in the emerald brilliance of her eyes. 'You want this,' he grated harshly. 'We both want this.'

She told herself she would have denied it—but she would never know. Because the answer she had begun falteringly to frame was obliterated by the heady power of his kiss as he drove his mouth down hard on hers. And was this so very wrong? To give in to something it had nearly killed them to deny themselves in the past?

Hard and punishingly, he plundered her lips—and never had a kiss so overwhelmed him, leaving him weak and dizzy, like a man who had dragged himself out of the water after swimming too long.

Was that groan his? And that sigh—was that his too?

But even while his big body shuddered with unstoppable desire his response angered him. Which buttons did she always press which so weakened him—he, a man who neither needed nor wanted anyone? His anger transmuted itself into a desire to show her exactly that. To give her a coldly efficient demonstration of his sexual powers.

He dragged his mouth away from hers and brushed it over her neck. Her head tipped back as he did so, and the ponytail of her fiery hair dangled behind her. He wrapped it around his wrist like a bright, silken rope. His other hand reached for her breast, splaying possessively over the silk-covered curve and feeling the nipple peak and harden beneath his questing fingers.

'Cesare!' she cried.

'What is it, *cara*? Is that good?'

'It's… It's… Oh, Cesare.' She wanted to call him darling—her darling—her sweet and wonderful and beautiful darling—Cesare. But he wasn't her darling, was he? Not any more. He was just a proud and angry man who was setting her on fire with the mastery of his touch.

'I should have done this years ago,' he ground out,

and pushed her back against the table, brushing aside all the papers and sliding her bottom onto the cleared space, scarcely aware of what he was doing, only that he was being driven on by a power greater than himself. 'And then I could have rid myself of your face. Rid myself of your pale, beautiful body. Taken the memory of you and screwed it up into a tiny ball and tossed it onto the fire.'

That didn't sound like affection—it sounded like the very opposite. Almost as if he despised her. Resented her. It should have killed her desire stone-dead—so why was it only escalating? 'Maybe you should—'

'Should what?'

'Stop what you're doing,' she breathed.

'But you don't want me to stop, do you?'

'Cesare—'

'*Do* you? You would kill me if I stopped, wouldn't you, my haunting green-eyed witch? You would rake those talons down over my bare back and draw blood, and then you would suck it off, like a vampire.'

'Yes! No!' No—no, of course she didn't want him to stop, and the visual imagery of his words almost made her faint. He was right. She had wanted this to happen since for ever, and even before that. 'Do it,' she whispered. 'Do it and get it over with. And then leave *me* with the peace that you so obviously crave, too.'

'Oh, don't worry,' he vowed furiously. 'I intend to.'

The skirt was tricky, but there wasn't a skirt in the world which would have defeated Cesare di Arcangelo.

Never had his experienced hands trembled so much. He rucked it up over her knees, and then further still, to reveal hold-up stockings clinging to pale thighs, and he sucked in a ragged breath, his resolve almost leaving him, but not quite.

Now he could see the fine triangle of lace which hinted at the soft red-gold tangle of hair beneath, and he touched her there with ruthless precision—lightly grazing his finger against her moist heat so that she cried out.

'Shut up!' he bit out. 'We don't want any of the secretaries coming in. There is only going to be one woman coming, and it is going to be you, my beauty.'

'Oh, Cesare,' she whispered helplessly.

He skated his fingers over the cool silk of her inner thigh and she writhed restlessly, impatiently—Cesare knew then that he had her completely in his power, but that he must use that power wisely.

For once he gave her the orgasm her body was so badly craving might she not just turn around and tell him to go to hell?

His fingers stilled and she groaned.

Or would it make her more compliant if he satisfied her now?

He needed her co-operation just as badly as he wanted to have sex with her if his scheme were to succeed. Wouldn't leaving her wanting him more make her much more acquiescent to his wishes? For hunger was one of life's great motivators, and sexual hunger the most powerful of all...

He thought of all the times he had pulled back from the brink that long, hot summer, and it gave him the strength to resist pulling her panties right off and plunging into her there and then.

But she writhed her hips again, giving a little whimpering sound of something fast approaching pain, and Cesare knew that she was past the point of no return. His smile was cruel and triumphant as he acted quickly, swiftly disentangling from her to stride across the room and lock the door. And then he came back and began to unbutton her blouse, and suddenly his triumph became a kind of submission.

'Oh, *cara*,' he groaned as he peeled away the silk to reveal the twin thrust of her lush breasts encased in pure white lace. Like a virgin, he thought helplessly, and bent his head to suckle her through the lace, feeling her buck wildly beneath him.

Blindly, he felt for her again, his hand sliding up her skirt and finding her damp warmth, and suddenly he wanted to taste it. Taste her. He tugged at her panties and she lifted her bottom as he edged them down, over her knees and past her ankles, until they dropped to the floor.

She was positioned perfectly, he realised as he began to trace the tip of his tongue up over her stockings to where lace became skin and then beyond, where the skin was softest of all and exquisitely sensitive. And then the folds themselves—moist, warm, secret entrances to her most honeyed treasure. He felt the tip with a touch so light it was almost a whisper, and he felt her little shudder of disbelief. He moved his tongue, curling the very edge of it around her in a rapid little circular movement which had her groping wildly for his shoulders, tangling her fingers frantically in his hair and crying his name out until he shushed her.

Even before he felt a rush of sweet moistness against his lips he could sense her release, and he held her hips while she began to shudder against his mouth. And then he moved away to take her in his arms, pressing his fingers hard against her while she convulsed around them, and he kissed away her wild cry until—to his astonishment—the cry became real. And tears, great shimmering tears, began to roll down her cheeks. He felt them mingling with their merged mouths—so many different flavours of her—and heard the choking little noises she made as she tried to recover herself.

He drew back from her, his black eyes hooded—for he never trusted women's tears. They turned them on and off at will, as weapons of manipulation, that was all. As a deterrent they could not have come at a better time, though, for they stilled his own sexual hunger so that he was able to rein it in—a feat of self-control which few other men would have been able to manage under the circumstances.

'You cry?' he demanded. 'I do not please you?'

It was an absurd question to ask—for surely he must have known that he had? Sorcha felt hopeless—helpless, shaky and insecure, and completely out of her depth—as if he had scraped away the top layer of skin

and left her raw and vulnerable, unsure what to do next.
She shook her head.

He smoothed her hair away from her damp face and
frowned. 'What is it?'

'That… That…'

She looked almost *shy,* he realised. *Shy?*

'What?'

She felt the blush wash upwards from her neck and
she opened her eyes, biting her lip. 'It was just… Oh!
With your tongue… Well, I mean, I've never…'

He held her still. Were his ears deceiving him.
'Never?' he demanded shakily.

She shook her head.

For a moment Cesare stilled, and then he buried his
face in her hair, closing his eyes. It was like music to
his ears, though he scarcely dared to believe it. Had she
hungered for him so badly over all these years that there
had been no other man for her?

He slid his arms around her waist and levered her
back up, smoothing her hair and looking into her eyes.
'You're trying to tell me you're a virgin?'

There was a split-second silence, and Sorcha was so
tempted to lie. To tell him what he really wanted to
hear—and wouldn't that make it much easier to bear?
Then the way that she'd reacted might have been a bit
more understandable—if she'd loved and wanted and
waited all that time for him to make love to her then who
could blame her for what she had just allowed to happen?

But she couldn't lie. Not to Cesare. And certainly not

about something as important as that. She knew how highly he rated purity—wasn't it the main reason he had asked her to marry him?

'No, I'm not a virgin,' she said quietly.

Now she had made him into a fool! Or had he only himself to blame for the sudden leap of hope he had felt? As if she wouldn't have had a long line of lovers...not when he knew how instantly she reacted to a man's touch.

His mouth curved. 'Your lovers must not have been good lovers,' he drawled. 'If they did not know how much a woman likes to be eaten.'

'You are disgusting!' she breathed.

'You weren't saying that a minute ago.'

Distractedly, she tugged at her skirt and straightened her blouse over her swollen breasts. It was like waking up from a dream when she hadn't even realised she'd been asleep.

What the hell would he think of her now?

Yet *he* had started it—set the ball rolling with that almost punishing kiss. *And you let him. Egged him on. Incited him in a way which was almost wanton.* Was it any excuse to say that she hadn't been able to stop herself? That once she had felt Cesare's lips on hers it had been like falling down a well straight into paradise?

She ran her tongue over her parched lips. 'That should never have happened,' she said hoarsely.

'Shouldn't it?'

Briefly, she closed her eyes. 'Not at the office!'

Cesare bit back a little murmur of satisfaction. The location had only added to its allure—but it was neither the time nor the place to tell her that her sudden capitulation to his kiss and its subsequent repercussions had been among the most erotic things to happen to him in a lifetime of erotic situations. That piece of knowledge would make her a little too powerful, and *he* liked to be the one with all the power.

And what was it about her that she should weave such magic over him even now? Because his desire for her had eaten away at him over the years? Or because she was so unexpectedly responsive? He swallowed down the bitter taste of jealousy—for that would not further his cause. He wanted her, and he intended to have her, and angry accusations about the men before him would not help his cause. And why should he feel jealousy over a woman for whom he felt nothing?

'And what about you?' she whispered, suddenly aware of how selfish she must seem—as if her own pleasure was the only thing which counted. This might not be a love affair made in heaven, but Cesare must be going out of his mind with frustration. 'Don't you…? Don't you…want…?'

'Sorcha—do not look so fraught. Let us acknowledge what we have—the chemistry between us is *incredibile*,' he murmured. 'Of course I want you—but I do not want our first time to be marred by a lack of time. By wondering if the phone will ring or one of the secretaries will knock on the door. Yes?' He lifted her onto the ground, enjoying the scarlet flush to her cheeks. He lifted her chin with his finger. 'Yes?' he said again.

His words only reinforced how *stupidly* she had behaved—without even a thought of what this could do to her career. This was the career she had sacrificed so much for, was it? She could afford to throw it away—along with her self-respect—just because sexy Cesare di Arcangelo had touched her?

She pushed his arm away. 'This is crazy,' she whispered.

'Crazy?' He gave a slow smile. 'That is not the definition I would have used, *mia bella*. It was *stupore*—amazing. And it is going to be amazing again. In fact, it's going to happen in my hotel room tonight. You know it is.'

He silenced her protest with a finger placed over the soft cushion of her lips, and she could smell her own raw scent on him and her eyes closed helplessly.

And when he took the finger away, she did not argue with him.

CHAPTER SIX

SORCHA'S mobile began to ring, and her green eyes narrowed as she looked at the unknown number. Cesare. She would bet money on it.

Cesare.

After he had gone off to meet Rupert, she had been completely distracted by what had taken place in the boardroom. Had that been his intention? To show off his sexual wizardry and rub in exactly what she'd been missing out on? Hoping perhaps to reduce her to a shivering jelly—as she lived out that erotic encounter, moment by moment? Was he also hoping that she would be unable to work properly so he could tell her that she was no longer required by the company? Perhaps his bizarre idea about having her front the Whittakers advertising campaign was nothing more than a double bluff?

No. Cesare might be underhand and devious—but she doubted whether even he would stoop so low as that.

But she had to claw back some of her self-control—to show him that she wasn't just some malleable female he

could twist and pull like one of those rubber cartoon char-
acters she'd used to play with as a child. She pulled the
sheet of figures she'd been working on towards her, so that
at least she was properly armed with a few facts in case he
tried to interrogate her about how she'd spent her day.

She cleared her throat and clicked the button. 'Sorcha
Whittaker.'

'Hello, Sorcha Whittaker,' purred the rich Italian accent
down the tinny line of the mobile. 'What are you doing?'

Had he guessed she'd been thinking about him—or
was this just par for the course with a man like Cesare?
She swallowed, closing her eyes, trying to rid her mind of
the image of his dark, mocking face—the feel of his mouth
against hers and his hands brushing against her skin.

How had this happened when it had never happened
to her before? That a man could start making love to you
and suddenly you couldn't stop thinking about him.

In the intervening hours he had obsessed her. It was
as if he pervaded her every thought and action—as if
nothing she could look at in her immediate surround-
ings would not remind her of Cesare.

'I've been working,' she said.

'How very disappointing. I thought you'd be thinking
about what I was doing to you a few hours ago,' he said
softly. 'I know that I have.'

'Cesare—don't.'

He leaned against the wall of the Whittakers factory,
alone now that the last of the staff had just trooped off
home for the day. 'But it should be interesting to see

what you've come up with. I'll pick you up at seven. We are having dinner tonight, remember?'

He had said nothing about dinner—he had merely intimated sex in his apartment. Sorcha shivered. With distance between them it suddenly seemed easier to say no.

'I don't know if it's such a good idea,' she said quietly.

There was a pause. 'You haven't changed, have you, Sorcha? You still like to tease men until they're going out of their mind. Promising, and then failing to deliver.'

The accusation hit her like a poison dart—but didn't some of what he'd said ring true? She could not take what she wanted from him like a greedy child and then back away, scared that she was going to get hurt. But if she didn't want to get hurt then she was going to have to protect herself—and that meant ruthlessly eradicating the side of her that wanted to beg him to be sweet to her, to pretend that he really cared for her. Because if there was no pretence, then she wouldn't start building up any foolish hopes, only to have them shattered by the harsh hammer of reality.

'Actually, I wasn't attempting to tease you at all,' she said coolly. 'I was speaking the truth, if you must know—I really *don't* think it's such a good idea. But that doesn't mean I'm not going to come.'

His relief that she wasn't backing off was only heightened by her cool response, and Cesare closed his eyes and bit back a sensual retort, recognising that he was skating on very thin ice—and that she was unpredictable. But if she thought that adopting an air of faint resignation meant that he might relent and call the whole thing off then she had underestimated him very badly indeed. She owed him—in more ways than one.

'I will pick you up at seven,' he said.

'Make it seven-thirty.'

He was left staring at the phone after she had severed the connection, and it occurred to him that he simply wasn't used to being left hanging on. Goodbyes to women he was intimate with were invariably protracted, with Cesare usually coming up with the let-out clause: *I have to go. Someone's trying to get through to me.* And then he would receive a breathless apology or a pouting little protest on the lines of *Oh, Cesare—you're always so busy!*

But he was only busy when he chose to be. He had reached a position of power and authority when it was always possible to delegate. These days he cherry-picked his jobs with the same ruthlessness which had taken him to the very top of the tree.

He had inherited much from his overambitious mother and father—including a need to make it in his own line of business, despite the vast amount of wealth he had inherited after their deaths.

His eyes narrowed suddenly as he glanced around the empty car park and the concrete jungle beyond, inexplicably comparing the scene with his orchards back home in Italy, and suddenly he felt a great pang of homesickness.

He drew out a set of keys from his pocket and looked up at the sky. By travelling the world he was missing all the seasons, he realised—the natural pace of the world was passing him by.

He thought about the August crop of damsons which grew in the gardens of his villa. About how they became so plump and ripe that they tumbled from the trees— glowing on the grass like purple jewels with succulent golden flesh inside. They would be out soon, he realised.

How long since he had bitten into their sweetness and let their juice run over his lips? How long since he had given himself time to gather in the harvest?

And why had this place suddenly made him start thinking about home? Cesare frowned as he thought about the rural retreat he'd bought as an antidote to the cold splendour of the Roman mansion in which he had spent a lonely childhood.

I need sex, he thought, as he loosened his tie and headed towards his car. Just sex.

And tonight you are going to get it, he thought with a slow smile of satisfaction as he climbed in behind the steering wheel of his sports car.

Sorcha stared out of the window to the front lawn, where a peacock was strutting and fanning its deep shiny turquoise feathers, squealing like a newborn baby.

Her hand fluttered to her throat to play with the pearl which hung from a fine golden chain, and she could feel a pulse beating at the base of her neck. It was almost as if she needed to touch herself to check that she was real—for she felt curiously detached, as though this evening was happening to someone who wasn't really Sorcha Whittaker, someone who had taken over her body for a while.

Because the real Sorcha Whittaker didn't have gasping orgasms across the boardroom table from a man she was certain despised her. Nor would the real Sorcha Whittaker have changed her outfit four times this evening until she was sure she had struck just the right balance.

Except that she still wasn't sure she had made the right choice, and there was no opportunity to try another because the long silver bonnet of Cesare's car was nosing its way up the long gravel drive.

The bell rang, and she ran downstairs and opened the door to see Cesare standing there, his head slightly to one side. He had taken his tie off, but otherwise he looked the same as he had done at work—save for a hint of dark shadow at his jaw.

With the evening sun behind him his olive skin looked almost luminous, and his thick hair was as darkly glossy as one of the ravens which sometimes strutted across the lawn before being chased away by the peacocks.

'Hello,' she said, and suddenly she felt confused. This felt like a date, and yet she was damned sure it wasn't a date. It was nothing more than a sexual liaison—a settling of old scores. But she felt as shy as a woman might feel on a first date—and that was even more peculiar—because how could any woman in her right mind feel shy after what had happened between them today?

Maybe because she *wasn't* in her right mind.

Cesare's eyes flickered over her. She was wearing some floaty dress in layers of green, with tiny little gold discs sewn into the fabric, her hair was loose down her back and she wore gold strappy sandals to flatter her bare brown legs. 'Pretty dress,' he murmured.

'Thank you.'

'You're ready?' He could see the wary expression in her eyes as she followed him out to the car and he told himself that it was inappropriate to ravish her on the doorstep—particularly since her mother and her brother might be around. Of course they might not be—but if he asked, then it would make him sound…

As if he was abusing the hospitality they had offered yesterday—just as they had offered all those years ago?

But it was actually more complex than that—because Cesare realised that he hadn't taken memories into account. He hadn't realised that they were such a powerful trigger into feeling things you didn't want to feel—until you reminded yourself that memories were always distorted by time. They had to be. They weren't constant—because no two people's memories were ever the same, were they?

Yet being with Sorcha like this mimicked a time when life had felt so simple and sweet—when he had felt unencumbered by anything other than the long, hot summer and the slow awakening of his senses.

But there was that distortion again—because that hadn't been part of Sorcha's agenda, had it? While he had been handling her with kid gloves she had been leading him on—playing with him with the clumsy confidence of a child who had mistaken a tiger-cub for a kitten. And she was just about to discover what it was really like in the jungle...

'Music?' he questioned, once they had strapped themselves into the car.

Sorcha sank into the soft leather of the seat. 'If you like.'

He slid a CD into the player as the car pulled away in a spray of gravel, but Sorcha almost wished she could tell him to turn it off again as the most heart-breakingly beautiful music swelled up and resonated through the air, so that you could hear nothing else but the voice and the song.

It was a man, singing in Italian, and she couldn't understand a word of it—but maybe she didn't need to. All she knew was that it was the most beautiful and sad song she had ever heard. It made her think of love and loss—and pain and happiness—and the man beside her. Sorcha closed her eyes.

She had to pull herself together—because it was pointless to feel things which would only be thrown back in her face, to want things which could never be hers.

Cesare glanced down at the hands which were

clasped in the lap of her dress—at the way her fingers interlocked, the way they gripped when the music reached a crescendo—and he bit down on his mouth, hard, in an effort to dispel his own frustration.

Because unless he stopped imagining himself pulling over into a lay-by and slipping his fingers between her legs, this was going to be a very long and uncomfortable drive.

The car drew up outside the only hotel in the village—the Urlin Arms, which was run by a slightly dotty ex-admiral who rated eccentricity over efficiency. It was his old family home, which had been converted, and the fact that the place had 'character' compensated in a small way for the constant stream of junior staff who were always flouncing out in a huff and leaving the Admiral in the lurch.

'You know this place?' asked Cesare as he opened the car door for her.

She clambered out of the low car and stood beside him, looking up at it. 'Yes. Of course. I remember when it was first converted.'

'Do you like it?'

'I love it. It's just…'

'Surprising that I've chosen to stay here?' he observed wryly.

'A bit.'

His black eyes mocked her. 'You thought I would have rented a glass and chrome extravaganza in London, did you?'

'Why, Cesare—are you a mind-reader?'

'No, I'm just good at reading body language,' he murmured. 'Especially yours.'

But Sorcha's poise was in danger of slipping as she followed him inside—where the Admiral was having his customary gin and tonic and regaling a tyre salesman from Humberside with the problems in the modern Navy.

'Evening, Admiral,' said Sorcha, forcing a smile and hoping that he was as man-of-the-world as he always claimed and wouldn't mention to her mother or Rupert that she'd been caught sneaking up to a hotel bedroom with Cesare di Arcangelo.

Why?

Because it felt wrong?

Because he was her boss?

They went upstairs to where he had obviously rented the best room. There were some fine pieces of furniture—a grandfather clock with a sonorous chime, a beautiful sandalwood chest, and faded silk rugs sprawled on polished floorboards.

Sorcha walked in and felt frozen to the spot, not sure what she was expected to do or say as Cesare pushed the door shut and leaned on it, studying her. And then his eyes narrowed and he turned and began walking towards a wooden drinks cabinet. 'Drink?' he called over his shoulder.

'Drink?' she echoed blankly.

He reappeared at the door. 'Wine? Or did you think

I was going to leap on you as soon as you set foot inside the door?'

Sorcha swallowed. 'How would I know? I've never been in this kind of situation before.'

Their eyes clashed. 'Me neither,' he said softly.

Some of the tension eased out of her. 'Wine, please.' She walked around the room, picking things up without really looking at them, trying not to look nervous when inside her stomach was tied up in knots.

Cesare came over and handed her a glass of red wine.

'Thanks.' She sipped it, and then took a bigger mouthful. 'Gosh—it's delicious. The Admiral must have better taste than I thought!'

He smiled. 'Actually, it's mine. My wine, that is. It is made from grapes which are grown in my own vineyard. The vines will be growing heavy now—with great clusters of grapes growing darker under the sun.'

His voice was dreamy enough to hurt, and suddenly Sorcha couldn't bear it. If she had married him she would have been mistress of those vineyards, too—as proud of their yield as he was—while instead she was standing awkwardly in a slightly scruffy hotel room, making small-talk while the real agenda simmered away unspoken. The elephant in the sitting room.

She put her glass down with a hand which she was suddenly afraid was going to start shaking. And he must not sense her reservations or her nervousness—because that would surely tell a man as clever as Cesare that she was vulnerable. If he thought that this was simply about a powerful sexual attraction which had never been properly explored then wouldn't she be safe? Maybe she would. For when they had taken their fill of one another perhaps they would discover that nothing remained.

She curved him a smile—a deliberately provocative smile she had no memory of ever smiling before. Where did a smile like that come from? Did you learn it from watching films? she wondered. Or was there just a moment in life when you met the only man for whom it was appropriate?

Cesare put his glass down beside hers, and for a moment he just savoured the anticipation of what was about to happen. At last. At *last*.

And then he beckoned to her. '*Venuta*,' he said softly, and held his arms out. '*Venuta, cara mia.*'

She did as he told her, went into them and felt them tighten round her. His breath was expelled from him in a hiss—like air being released from a pressure cooker.

'Cesare,' she breathed, on a note which sounded broken.

And that was when he began to kiss her. Her arms fastened around his neck as hungrily she pressed her body closer to his—and as he kissed her he began pushing up the filmy dress. Up over her bare thighs, his fingers luxuriating as they kneaded the soft flesh, as if they were reacquainting themselves with an old friend.

And Sorcha realised that she could not play passive. Not this time. This was the command performance—for one night only! Remember that, she urged herself. Don't

be lulled by sweet sensation and unrealistic wishes just
because his lips are soft and his kiss passionate enough
to make you start indulging in make-believe.

She slid her hand between his legs and he groaned.
Gently, she rubbed her palm down over the hard heat of
his arousal and the pressure of his kiss increased—until
he drew his head away, his black eyes looking as opaque
and distant as a man in the midst of a fever.

'You think I am going to do it to you here?' he questioned unsteadily. 'Is that what you want? You are one
of those women who like it any place except in bed?'

One of those women. He might as well have slapped
her. Sorcha shook her head. 'No,' she breathed.

He scooped her up without warning and carried her
through into the bedroom, laid her down on the bed—
and perhaps he sensed that his words had been clumsy,
for he started to stroke her and soothe her, and anoint
her skin with feather-light kisses, and speak to her in
words of soft Italian.

He worked her up into such a pitch of longing that
Sorcha was barely aware of the gauzy drapes which fell
in soft folds over the imposing four-poster bed. Quite
honestly it could have been a bare mattress on the floor
of a downtown apartment she wanted him so much—
and suddenly she was tearing at his shirt, pulling at it
in a frenzy.

He started laughing as a button went bouncing across
the floorboards, but he lifted a shoulder to help her
shrug him out of it, and when his chest was bare she

touched it wonderingly, curling her fingers in the dark whorls of hair which grew there.

'You are hungry? Like a tiger?' he murmured.

But his laugh grew slightly unsteady as she unzipped him, pulling off his trousers as best she could and murmuring as she skated her fingertips over the dark silk of his boxers.

His eyes snapped open. 'Don't,' he warned.

'Or what?' she questioned breathlessly.

'Or this.' It was time to take back control—before he was fooled into mistaking this unique situation for something else. With a fluent efficiency born out of years of practice he peeled her dress off and tossed it aside, then unclipped her bra and sent it across the room in a lazy arcing movement. And then, with a hard smile of enjoyment, he caught the fabric of her mint-green panties between his hands and ripped them apart.

Sorcha's mouth dried and her eyes widened. 'Cesare—'

'Do you know how many times I've fantasised about doing that?' he grated as he pulled her down onto the bed, peeling off his boxers as he bent over to straddle her. 'And this?' he whispered, as he cradled his erection and pushed it close to her.

He paused only to reach for a condom, which it seemed he had conveniently placed ready beforehand, and Sorcha began to get a terrible feeling of panic. This wasn't how it was supposed to be. Oh, she had known exactly what was going to happen, and her body was crying out for him, but it all seemed so…so…*mechanical.*

All those dreams she had cherished were about to be dealt a fatal blow. But maybe that was best—it was only forbidden and impossibly perfect dreams which made it impossible to move on. Reality was a much safer beast.

He felt her tension and kissed her with slow deliberation until he felt all her apprehensiveness dissolve—even though the effort it took nearly killed him. 'I want you,' he ground out. 'And I want you now.'

'You've…you've got me.'

He entered her slick tightness and he was lost—as if he had found himself in the middle of the sea and a mist had come down so that he couldn't see any more, could only feel.

And—*Madre di Dio*—could he feel her! For a moment he felt shaken by the power of each perfect thrust.

Was she doing okay? she wondered as feverishly she kissed his shoulder. Was it acceptable for her to float away on this sensual bubble? Because it had never felt like this before—never, never, never.

Like an adult who had just got back on a horse after years of abstinence, Sorcha tried to remember the moves which pleased most, and she wrapped her ankles around his back and writhed her hips.

For a moment he froze. He looked down at her and his eyes were black, almost…hostile.

'What? What is it, Cesare?'

'Oh, but you are…good, *cara,*' he said unevenly. 'Very good. I thought you would be.'

So why did it sound like an insult? And why did something alter from that moment? The pitch and intensity of his movements changed, and he drove into her like a man who had been starved of sex all his life. You and me both, she thought. And—even though she tried to fight it—she felt herself swept away by the longest and most powerful orgasm of her life.

She was still crying out helplessly against his shoulder when Cesare followed, with one final deep thrust which sent him spinning off into a place of unbearable sweetness. It seemed to take him a long time to return to earth.

After it was over he lay back against the bed, staring upwards at the ceiling of a bedroom that wasn't his, oddly shaken by what had just happened. But that was because he had waited so long, he told himself—and now that the wait was over the hunger and the passion would die a natural death.

He turned to look at Sorcha. Her bright hair was tumbled across his pillow and her skin was rose-pink. But her eyes were closed.

'Are you sleeping?' he questioned softly.

Behind the sanctuary of her closed lids, Sorcha composed herself before opening them. Act like you don't care, she told herself.

'No.'

His eyes narrowed as he searched her face, but it was blank, like an unpainted canvas—as if she felt nothing.

Yet how could that be? Even if she no longer had any great affection for him, he was experienced enough to know that her orgasm had been of the bone-melting variety. Cesare prided himself on giving a woman plea-sure—indeed, it often inspired an almost slavish devotion in his lovers. Compliments were his due, and always effusive. Always. But not, it seemed, from Sorcha. He traced a finger along her shoulder and she shivered. 'You liked that, *cara?*'

Keep it real, she told herself. Protect yourself. He must know how good he is. 'It was…' Sorcha shrugged. 'It was okay.'

For a moment his face darkened. 'You mean you were *faking it?*' he demanded in disbelief.

Sorcha started laughing. 'I'm not *that* good an actress.'

He relaxed. 'Ah, I see—you are teasing me?'

'Aren't you used to being teased, then, Cesare?'

He pulled her closer. 'Not,' he said silkily, 'at moments like these.' Women tended to idolise him. His ego was vast, but it was not self-delusion which made him sometimes feel like a trophy—not when he knew that women sometimes boasted of having been his lover. Lately he had found the very obvious conquests a bore. He looked down at Sorcha's bright hair. Yet she had been the easiest conquest of all. Or had she? He felt a twist of inexplicable pain.

'You have had many other lovers?' he demanded.

She turned her face towards him and her green eyes were serious. 'Do you ask every woman that?'

GET FREE BOOKS and FREE GIFTS
WHEN YOU PLAY THE...

777

Lucky 7

SLOT MACHINE GAME!

Just scratch off the silver box with a coin. Then check below to see the gifts you get!

YES!
I have scratched off the silver box. Please send me the 2 free Harlequin Presents® books and 2 free gifts for which I qualify. I understand I am under no obligation to purchase any books, as explained on the back of this card.

306 HDL EF37   **106 HDL EF4Y**

FIRST NAME	LAST NAME

ADDRESS

APT.#	CITY

STATE/PROV.	ZIP/POSTAL CODE

7	7	7	**Worth TWO FREE BOOKS plus 2 BONUS Mystery Gifts!**
🍒	🍒	🍒	**Worth TWO FREE BOOKS!**
♣	♣	♣	**Worth ONE FREE BOOK!**
🔔	🔔	🍒	**TRY AGAIN!**

www.eHarlequin.com

(H-P-12/06)

Offer limited to one per household and not valid to current Harlequin Presents® subscribers.

Your Privacy - Harlequin Books is committed to protecting your privacy. Our Privacy Policy is available online at www.eHarlequin.com or upon request from the Harlequin Reader Service. From time to time we make our lists of customers available to reputable firms who may have a product or service of interest to you. If you would prefer for us not to share your name and address, please check here ☐.

'Of course I do not. But it is different with you.'

'Why?' she whispered.

Because I wish I'd been the first. Because I cannot bear the thought of another man doing to you what I have just done. 'Just curiosity.'

'But it's none of your business, is it?' she asked sweetly. 'I haven't asked you how many women *you've* had.'

Cesare felt wrong-footed. 'That is different,' he said stubbornly.

'*Another* thing that's different? My, my, Cesare— where were you when women got the vote?'

He could feel a mixture of exasperation and frustration, because she still hadn't answered his question. 'You were right,' he said suddenly. 'We could never have been married. For I could never have tolerated a woman with strong opinions such as yours, which often do not coincide with my own.'

'Then everything has turned out for the best, hasn't it? Of course if we'd married my opinions would have been different,' she said. 'Because you would have helped form them.'

'And you think that would have been such a terrible thing?' he demanded, even though deep-down he admired her independence of thought.

There was a pause. She knew that there was an easy answer to give—but what would be the point? This— whatever it was they had between them—was not destined to last, so why not be honest at least? 'Well, yes—I do. Because then all I would have been was an extension of you—with no intellectual freedom of my own.'

It was one of the things he now found so exhilarating about her company—this feisty and challenging mind she had developed. But surely to admit that—even to himself—would represent a loss of face? 'And that is why you will never find a husband!' he stormed.

Sorcha stared at him, and then started laughing. 'I can't believe that a sophisticated man of the world just came out with something as crass as that!' But her laughter died when she saw the sudden dark look of intent on his face.

'In the bedroom a man is just a man, *cara mia*—and his response is rather more…*primitive*. And that is the double-edged sword—because the kind of man who turns you on is precisely the kind of man who will not tolerate your need for independence and freedom.'

'Cesare…' She wanted to say *Don't*. But she couldn't, because her body was craving his once more. And maybe he was right—maybe she *was* doomed to want what she could never have. An alpha-man who could never accept the woman she really was.

'Nothing to say, *cara?*' Luxuriously, he splayed his hands over the silken globes of her bottom and bent his mouth to her ear. 'Then let me say it for you… In the end, all the things you claim to want count for nothing, because you cannot resist the demands of your body. And though the spirit is willing, the flesh is very weak.

If I had asked you objectively whether you wished to find yourself in my bed, you would have answered no—and yet here you are. It must distress you sometimes to acknowledge that your sexual drive is so strong.'

She stared up at him, the hurt shimmering in her eyes. 'You think I react like this with every man? That I let anyone do what you did to me in the office this afternoon?'

A slow smile of satisfaction spread over his face. 'You mean it is just me?' he murmured.

Sorcha felt as if she'd walked into a silken trap and he had nearly tricked her into giving him the answer he wanted.

Suddenly she wanted to hurt him back—to lash out at him the way he'd been doing ever since he'd come back into her life.

'You want to slot me in as yet another of your damned stereotypes, don't you?' she stormed. 'Where once I was your precious virgin, now I'm a loose woman. But how loose? That is the question. How many men will you decide I've slept with, Cesare? Ten? Twenty? A hundred?'

'Stop it, Sorcha,' he said suddenly, as the mental pictures her angry words conjured up became unbearable.

'Then stop judging me by your archaic standards! Do you want to know how many?'

'No.'

'You don't?'

His eyes glittered. 'I just want to know if any of them were as good as me.'

She stared at him. 'You are unbelievable.'

'So I'm told. I'll take that as a no.' He kissed her and then lifted his head, an arrogant thrill curving his lips as he stared down at her rumpled, rosy beauty. 'I want to see you smile. Ah, *that* is better.' He stroked his hand down over her waist and felt her shiver. 'Now I'm going to make love to you. And then…'

Sorcha swallowed as he traced his tongue along the curve of her jaw. He was tormenting her, teasing her, and yet she didn't want him to stop it, because his soft cajoling was more enticing than anything else. 'Then?' she whispered.

Cesare touched the tip of his tongue to her ear. 'I think we must discuss the campaign.'

Sorcha stared at him.

'I've made an appointment for you to see an old friend of mine,' he murmured. 'He has an exhibition starting in London.' His eyes glinted. 'He used to be one of the world's most famous photographers until he gave it up. But he's agreed to do this job as a favour. It is,' he finished with satisfaction, 'a very great honour.'

For a moment he might as well have been speaking in his native Italian. Sorcha jerked her head away and blinked at him.

'What are you talking about?'

'The new face of Whittakers. You.' He nodded to himself.

She sat upright in bed, bright hair streaming down over her bare breasts, suddenly finding that rage was a far easier emotion to live with than willing surrender. 'Excuse me, but I don't actually remember *agreeing* to do it.'

'Really?' He slid his hand between her legs. 'I thought you just had.'

Sorcha covered his hand with hers and halted its sensuous progress. 'Let's make one thing clear, Cesare,' she said. 'The sex is separate. I'm with you now because I want to be. Not because I'm allowing myself to be seduced into agreeing to have my photo taken.'

His eyes narrowed. 'You mean you're refusing to do the job?'

She gave him a demure smile. Oh, but she was enjoying this. Why didn't some enterprising person write a book on how empowering it was to defy a man who thought it his right to issue commands and have them instantly obeyed?

'That's not what I'm saying at all, Cesare,' she said patiently. 'I'll do it because I can see the sense in it. And if it works I'll be the first to pat you on the back—since that is so clearly what you like. But my decision has absolutely nothing to with your skill as a lover.' She saw the incredulous look in his black eyes and resisted a smile of triumph. 'And now—if you don't mind—I'd like you to drive me home.' She slid her legs over the side of the bed in a graceful movement which he followed with a kind of helpless hunger.

'Home?' he repeated, in a voice of strained disbelief.

'Please.'

'Do you mind telling me why?' he demanded.

Hearing the outrage in his voice, Sorcha lifted her head and steeled herself to meet the hot and sensual challenge which sizzled from his black eyes, reminding herself that sex appeal as powerful as Cesare's was a very dangerous thing. It made you want to mould yourself against his silken olive skin and be made love to until the stars faded from the sky. But that would be a disaster—and a recipe for tip-tilting her emotions so much that she wouldn't be able to think straight. And wasn't it bad enough already?

She recognised that she was still vulnerable around him. That just because she had had mind-blowing sex with him it didn't mean her heart had been granted some sort of special immunity from his spell. 'We'll have to be careful,' she said.

Cesare's eyes narrowed. 'Careful?'

Sorcha bit her lip. Did he think she was talking about contraception? Was that the only level his mind operated on? 'I want to keep this secret,' she elaborated. 'I don't want anyone finding out, and I assume that you don't either.'

'Oh, do you?' he questioned dangerously.

She had thought that this would please him. But the glitter in his eyes did not look like pleasure, and the steely note underpinning his stern voice did not sound like pleasure. 'Surely you agree with me, Cesare? For one thing it's highly unprofessional for two people working together to be...' She struggled to think of a suitable description, but the only one which came to mind wasn't even true. 'Intimate.'

There was a pause as he weighed up her words. 'But that's not the real reason you want to keep it secret, is it, Sorcha?' he asked softly. Yet inside Cesare was reeling. *He* was the one who usually laid down conditions within a relationship. Never before had a woman dared to impose her rules on him, and he wasn't sure he liked it.

For a moment there was another silence. 'No.'

He raised his dark brows. 'So, are you going to enlighten me, *cara?*'

And—despite all her intentions—Sorcha suddenly found that it took a lot of courage to articulate her fears, to face up to the truth, no matter how bitter the reality.

'Well, your position here is only temporary, and therefore if we embark on an affair it isn't destined to last—it's just a short-lived pleasure. We don't want anyone building it up into something it isn't.' She shrugged. 'And we don't want other people projecting emotions on us when it finishes. If they don't know about it—they can't.'

'You really have this all worked out, don't you?' he said admiringly.

'Kind of.' What choice did she have? What other way to protect herself against certain heartbreak?

She bent over to pick up her discarded bra and Cesare quickly shut his eyes in erotic agony. Was she deliberately tormenting him? Sliding the filmy lace garment over her breasts with all the sensual show of a stripper?

With a simmering fury he climbed out of bed, feeling as if she had wrong-footed him yet again.

'So really,' he said slowly, 'this strategy of yours is designed to thwart any hurt pride?'

Sorcha nodded, turning away from the temptation of his magnificent naked body. 'Surely you can understand that, Cesare?'

Pride? Oh, yes—he could understand that. He knew the pain and the comfort it could bring. If pride were a degree course at college, then Cesare would have picked up a first in it.

CHAPTER SEVEN

'OKAY, Sorcha—if you could stand just over *there*.'

Sorcha stood on the chalk cross the assistant was indicating while they held light meters up close to her face and wobbled sheets of white paper around the place. She had only been there half an hour, and already she was bored out of her mind. How did professional models manage it? she wondered, devoting yet more silent sympathy towards that breed of overpaid beanpoles, because at least it stopped her thinking about…

Wriggling her shoulders, she smiled at the assistant. She was *not* going to think about Cesare and the way he had assumed he could seduce her into doing any damned thing he pleased.

Still, at least in some things she had shown him that she had a mind of her own. Every time he had made love to her she had insisted on going home to sleep in her own bed, even though he had tried his best to make her stay. Even though he was…was…

She shivered and closed her eyes. Why remember the

way his lips had trailed a slow path from neck to belly and beyond? The way he had made her cry out in surrender, her back arching helplessly as he gave a low laugh of triumph?

Why think about that *now,* when she was trying to be strong as she prepared to have her photo taken, trying not to melt when she thought about his dark, irresistible face?

That was why her need to sleep apart from him was so urgent—so necessary—for who could predict what would happen in those strange, unreal hours before dawn, when you were lying so close to a man who had been part of your heart for so long? How difficult she might have found it not to cradle him in her arms and tenderly stroke his thick black hair—to tell him that he made her feel whole again.

And was it her fierce resolve which made Cesare seek to demonstrate *his* power over her in different ways? That if he could not have her at night, then he would avail himself of every other opportunity which came his way? Did he take more than erotic delight in seducing her again and again at the office, despite her breathless protestations that it felt wrong?

'It does not feel wrong to *me, cara,*' he had murmured as he'd pushed her back against the boardroom door and rucked her skirt up, and thrust into her long and hard and slow. 'It feels oh…so…right.'

And Sorcha had sobbed softly into his shoulder as he brought her to another shuddering orgasm, telling herself that she had only herself to blame for this surreptitiousness. That *she* was the one who had demanded it be kept secret.

That morning he had picked her up from the house to drive her to the photo-shoot, and during the drive she'd seemed to be aware of him in a way she never had been before.

As if even the strip of hair-roughened wrist which showed beneath the crisp, starched shirt-cuff with its gleaming golden cufflink was of endless fascination to her. As though she could have studied his skin for hours and never tired of it.

Was that because his collecting her was about as close as they had come to replicating a date?

But there had been no kiss to greet her, just an atmosphere of simmering tension in the car, which Sorcha had tolerated until she'd been able to bear it no longer.

'Is something wrong, Cesare?'

'Wrong?' He gave a short laugh. 'I want you so much that I can barely drive in a straight line—what could possibly be wrong?'

'I thought you would have worn yourself out yesterday,' she said tartly.

He shot her a glance. 'So did I,' he observed drily.

And in spite of everything, Sorcha's heart leapt with longing. 'Why don't you stop the car and kiss me?' she said softly.

'Because we're stuck on the M25, you're about to be photographed by a genius—and time is money,' he snapped frustratedly.

'Sorry,' said Sorcha automatically. *Good girl?* How did models *stand* it?

The studio was situated in the heart of London, in a large, nondescript basement which seemed to be buzzing with life and people. As well as the assistant, there was a stylist and *her* assistant, plus two representatives from the ad agency which represented the Whittakers account.

Everyone in the place was wearing some kind of denim—apart from Sorcha, who had been given a ghastly gingham apron to wear to promote the sauce and had *not* been expecting an audience.

'Can someone push that piece of tomato out of the way? Can you lift your head a fraction higher, Sorcha? No—a bit to the left!'

Sorcha's smile didn't falter, because she was determined to give it her best—even though she could very easily play the role of victim and claim that she had been forced into doing the shoot. Indeed, she could do it with such bad grace that she would be pronounced hopeless—and then the whole scheme would have to be rethought. *Then* there would be egg all over his gorgeous face.

As a way of getting back at Cesare it would be a masterly move. But getting back at him for *what?* For being autocratic? Because that was *him*—he was right— it was part of what attracted her to him as well as what ultimately made them incompatible.

She couldn't punish the man just because he was

making her feel stuff she didn't want to feel. You couldn't hold someone else responsible for *your* mood—because in the end that was all down to you.

There was a bustle and a buzz, and Sorcha looked round to see what all the fuss was about just as a man dressed entirely in black walked into the studio with Cesare directly behind him.

'Is that the photographer?' Sorcha whispered.

'You don't know?' The assistant looked at her as if she had just been beamed down from another planet. 'That's Maceo di Ciccio,' she said. 'And that's Cesare di Arcangelo with him—oh, but you know *him,* don't you? Didn't he bring you here?'

'He certainly did,' said Sorcha pleasantly.

Cesare gave her a cool look, and she sent him an equally cool one back, which made his eyes narrow in mocking response. But Sorcha knew that she was playing with fire. That the feelings she had had for him all those years ago hadn't just faded away into nothing. He still amused her and he still stimulated her, on far more than just a physical level—and that was where the danger lay.

Men were good at keeping things purely sexual, and women were notoriously bad at it. Even worse, sex brought out an emotional response in women which had the capacity to make them weak as kittens.

Well, that's not going to be *me,* she thought fiercely.

She watched as the photographer was greeted with reverence by all his acolytes, and Sorcha couldn't help thinking that Maceo di Ciccio was on the wrong side of the camera.

He was wearing black jeans and a fine cashmere sweater. His face was rugged—with harsh angles and slanting black eyes—but although his mouth was soft and sensual, there was an almost cruel curve at the edge of his lips. With his ruffled black hair, he looked a little like a buccaneer—the kind of man who would just go all out to get what it was he wanted. And, looking like that, she didn't imagine he had to try very hard.

Cesare watched while an assistant held a light meter under Sorcha's chin, and he wondered where his expected feeling of triumph had gone. He had got his way, because she was here—even though she didn't look as if she particularly wanted to be—and he had been enjoying some mind-blowing and no-strings sex with her into the bargain!

So what was the cause of the black mood which had enveloped him since he'd got out of bed that morning? Alone, after she'd damned well made him drive her home at some godforsaken hour. As usual.

And that was the irony—because he *liked* to sleep alone. He liked to wake up when he wanted, rather than have some female slipping out from beneath him, disturbing him while she went into the bathroom to clean her teeth and brush her hair in order to achieve that just-got-out-of-bed look.

Sometimes in the cold, cruel light of day it wasn't easy to make conversation, and the easy talk of the night before became stilted and formal. At night you had the cloak of darkness and the comfort of wine to take the edge off uncomfortable silences.

She had tied him up in knots yet again, and he damned well resented it!

'But she is beautiful,' Maceo suddenly murmured in Italian at his side. 'You told me she was a witch.'

Cesare looked at her, and a sudden unease prickled at his skin. 'Witches can be beautiful,' he drawled. Ignoring his friend's assessing expression, he leaned back against the wall to watch as Maceo walked across the studio towards her.

'*Ciao, bella,*' said Maceo softly, and Sorcha got the sudden intimation of being in the presence of a creative genius. Pulling off the cashmere sweater to reveal a black T-shirt beneath, he handed it to a waiting assistant and narrowed his eyes. 'So you are Sorcha, *si?*'

'Yes, that's me.' Sorcha smiled nervously. 'Um, you *do* know I'm not a professional model? In fact, I've never done anything but family snapshots in my life.'

'I can tell—but that is perfect,' he murmured. 'Just as *you* are perfect. I am not looking for the professional model, with her face just *so,* who tosses her head back—*so…*!'

He gave an exaggerated flick of his dark head and Sorcha giggled.

'That is good,' he said softly. 'I want you to laugh, for you must be….how do you say? *Saucy! Si,* for that is what Cesare wishes. For the sauce!'

All the assistants laughed sycophantically.

Across the other side of the studio, Cesare felt his face turning to stone. Since when had Maceo decided to ham up his Italian side—and *why*? Especially when Maceo's English was as good as his own. But he answered his own question when he saw Sorcha responding as if he was God's gift to women. Couldn't she see through all that hand-waving stuff?

Apparently not. Because now she was nodding her head energetically at something that the photographer was saying to her. Usually the two men formed a strong mutual admiration society, but suddenly Cesare felt like withdrawing his membership.

He had known Maceo since they were both five—when their two very different worlds had collided at a weekly judo class. Maceo had won a scholarship to study it, and it had been one of Cesare's many after-school activities, designed to keep him out of the house.

Maceo had risen from the slums and had had to claw his way up from the very bottom—perhaps that was what had helped give him his unique talent for seeing behind the masks that people presented. He had photographed models and princesses, queens and criminals—and then grown bored with it.

With the money he had earned, Maceo had bought an ailing fashion magazine and discovered that he had a talent for breathing new life into media ventures. These days he owned a TV station, several more magazines, and was proprietor of one of Italy's top-selling newspapers. He rarely took photos—only when the fancy took him. This favour to Cesare had amused him and been gladly given—so why the hell was Cesare now wishing that he had gone the more conventional route and employed someone that the ad agency had recommended?

And why was he feeling jealous of Maceo when Sorcha was a woman he was merely having sex with in order to finally get her out of his system?

Maceo smiled at her. 'You are ready, *bellezza?*'

Sorcha nodded—even though her heart was racing with nerves—feeling like a lamb headed for the slaughterhouse as she stood in front of the charismatic photographer. 'Ready as I'll ever be,' she gulped.

'Then come over here. Just here—you see? Just ignore the stylist—she paints the tomato with oil to make it look shiny. Relax, Sorcha. Just relax. *Si,* that is better. Now, put your finger in your mouth. Yes. That is perfect. Ah, *si!* You are perfect. *Bellezza!*'

A nerve flickered in Cesare's cheek.

He knew that in order to get the very best out of a subject Maceo was photographing it was necessary for the subject to relax. So why shouldn't Maceo call Sorcha beautiful, when that was nothing but the truth?

And why the hell was it eating him up?

Sorcha could feel her heart hammering. This was a *nightmare*—especially with Cesare standing in the shadows of the room, his silhouette looking so darkly forbidding. All she could see was the glitter of his eyes, but she could sense his disapproval as surely as if it were radiating in waves from his hard, lean body. And *who* was the one who had set this whole thing up?

Defiantly, she licked her lips and pouted.

'Now, look at me as you would look at your lover,' demanded Maceo.

This was harder, and stupidly Sorcha blushed. Was that because her lover was standing on the other side of the room, glowering at her? She heard a door slam, and when Sorcha looked up Cesare had gone.

'No, *cara*,' Maceo urged, as he followed the direction of her gaze. 'Not that look. Not the shy in-love smile, but the grown-up foxy smile. The look of a confident woman. Comfortable in her own skin—knowing that she gives pleasure as well as receives it.'

In a way it was better that Cesare *had* gone, because at least now Sorcha felt more able to deliver—if only to prove to herself and to Maceo that his assessment had been completely wrong. It had not been a shy in-love smile at all. Not at all. Because she wasn't in love with anyone.

She put her finger into her mouth, widened her eyes at the camera, and thought of Cesare, naked and luminous.

'*Perfetto!*' applauded Maceo.

She tilted her head coquettishly, looking as if she had just been told a delicious secret as she remembered the things he had whispered last night as he had thrust long and hard and deep inside her.

'*Meravigliosa!*' murmured Maceo.

Sorcha really started getting into it—tossing her head like a filly and meeting Maceo's enigmatic black eyes.

'Now you see why the models toss their heads…*so?*' he observed wryly.

He shot roll after roll of film, and by the time he'd finished Sorcha felt exhausted. She picked up her bag and jacket. Maybe modelling wasn't quite as easy as it appeared on the surface.

'Ah, there is Cesare,' murmured Maceo sardonically as they walked out into the reception area. 'With the sunny smile.'

Cesare was pacing the floor like a dark, caged tiger. He barely flicked her a glance, but directed his attention to Maceo.

'What the hell was *that* all about?' he questioned in Italian.

'Could you be a little more specific?' answered Maceo, in the same language.

'I asked you to take her photograph—not to try it on!'

'If I *had* been trying it on, then she'd be leaving with me,' boasted Maceo. 'If you can't hang on to your women, di Arcangelo—then don't take it out on me.'

The two men stood glaring at one another, and Sorcha had had quite enough. She marched out of the foyer and left them to it. Let Cesare travel back on his own—*she* would get the train!

She was halfway down Marylebone High Street when she heard a distinctive voice calling out her name and the sound of footsteps behind her. When she turned round, there was Cesare—his dark face a picture of barely repressed rage.

'Where do you think you're going?' he demanded.

'To the station! I wasn't going to hang around while you and Maceo had your Italian conversation class—I'd already had an exhausting morning.'

His mouth twisted. 'Yes, I could see that.'

The undertone of accusation in his voice was unmistakable. 'And what's that supposed to mean?'

'Do you think I am blind, Sorcha?' he asked hotly. 'I saw what was going on between you and Maceo.'

'Going on?' she choked. 'You mean the flirting, which I assume he does as automatically as breathing with every woman he photographs?'

'I know what kind of a man he is!' he declared. 'And the reputation he has with women. He does not know that there is anything between us, so why wouldn't he make a pass at you?'

'But there *is* nothing between us!' she flared. And didn't part of her just long for him to reject that assumption?

But Cesare didn't seem remotely interested in defining relationships—he was not letting up on the subject which interested him far more. 'You are saying that you didn't find him attractive?'

Sorcha sighed. This was difficult—but keeping her own emotions in check to lessen the risk of getting hurt did not mean that she couldn't be in some way honest about the way she felt.

'Under different circumstances, I suppose I might have done,' she said carefully.

His eyes narrowed. 'What kind of circumstances?'

If she had been a child, she would have stamped her foot. 'Oh, you can be so dense, Cesare! I thought I'd made it clear to you that just because I wasn't a virgin when I slept with you it doesn't necessarily follow that no man is safe from my advances! I don't deal with a multitude of partners at the same time.' She stared at him. 'Do you?'

'No.' There was a long silence while he stared at her, and suddenly some of the tension left him. Some, but not all. 'Am I going crazy?' he questioned softly.

'I don't know—are you?'

'Yes,' he groaned as he pulled her into his arms. He wanted to tell her that it wasn't supposed to be like this— he had thought he was going along in a straight line, yet he was encountering twists and turns all along the way.

'I find myself wanting to kiss green-eyed women in the middle of a busy street,' he murmured.

'Cesare—you can't.'

'Can't I?'

'Think of your reputation.'

'What about yours?'

Sorcha couldn't remember the last time she had been kissed in public. It didn't last long, and it wasn't one of those awful kisses which made other people feel sick— with the couple looking as if they were enjoying a three-course meal.

No, it was brief and hard and intense—in effect, it was a powerful stamp and a demonstration of Cesare's mastery, and when she drew back from it she was breathless, oblivious to the red double-decker bus which trundled by and the people who were turning to look at them.

'Now what?' she questioned.

'Let's find a hotel,' he said unsteadily.

CHAPTER EIGHT

SUNLIGHT streamed in through the windows and Sorcha sleepily opened her eyes and yawned. She had often wondered what kind of people spent the afternoon in bed in a hotel, and now she had discovered the answer.

People like her.

She glanced at the figure in the bed beside her. Cesare was sleeping, his magnificent body stretched out like an artist's model, the olive skin glowing against the rumpled tangle of white sheets. But while his muscular body was hard and lean, his face in repose had a curious softness about it. Thick black lashes formed two shadowy arcs, and the luscious mouth was curved into a sensual little pout.

How many beds had he lain in like this? she wondered. Had he spent anonymous afternoons in luxury hotels in all the major cities around the world? For this was a very different venue from the Urlin Arms, with its faded carpets and temperamental staff. Here the drapes were pure lined silk, the chandelier French, and the writing desk antique.

How many women? Did they all blur into one eager and giving body? In a year's time would he have to frown to remember just where it was he had stayed with her?

There was a glint from between his half-closed eyes, and a hand reached out to rest with easy familiarity on her thigh. How well sex could mock real intimacy, thought Sorcha with a pang.

'You look lost in thought,' he murmured.

'I was.'

'Are you going to share it?'

What an emotive word *share* could be—did he know that? Did women leap on it like hungry little puppies because it hinted at something beyond the communion of bodies which had just taken place?

'You won't want to hear.'

'Try me,' he murmured, stretching his legs and making no attempt to hide his renewed stirring of desire.

'I was wondering if you made a habit of this.'

'This?'

There he was—already playing for time! 'Having sex with women in anonymous hotel rooms.'

He studied her thoughtfully. 'What do you think? That every time I visit a city I pick up a beautiful woman and take her to bed?'

'Do you?'

He laughed. 'Once—a long time ago—I went through a stage of doing exactly that.' It had been when he had left her, when he had been hurting—not expecting to hurt, nor wanting to, as if he had a divine right to somehow be immune from the pain of relationships.

There had always been willing women—and at that time it had seemed that the supply of them was endless. It was almost as if his icy indifference had turned them on, providing them with the challenge that they might be the one to break through that cold heart to find the warmth of the man beneath. They never had, of course—and Cesare had turned away more than he had slept with. He had felt like a gorged child who had been given permission to spend the night in a sweetshop.

'It sounds like every man's idea of heaven,' said Sorcha, hoping that her voice didn't sound sour— because how he lived his life was his business, not hers.

'It wasn't,' he said flatly. 'Predictability is boring, and when something is so easy to get, it doesn't have the same value.'

Sorcha went very still. 'You didn't have to fight very hard to get *me* into bed,' she said in a small voice.

His voice was cool and mocking. 'You don't think so? This seduction actually started *seven* years ago— and, using those sums, I'd say that you were actually the hardest of all.' Black eyes hardened, became watchful. 'And what about you, Sorcha, since this seems to be true confession time?'

'What do you want to know? Actual numbers, like in that film—where I go through my conquests one by one and make you laugh?'

Laugh? He winced, knowing that the fierce stab of jealousy which shot through him was unreasonable—but then, he had never been accused of being a reasonable man.

'No,' he grated, and, unfolding his big, lean body, he got out of bed. 'Let's have a drink.'

Had he suggested that to distance himself? Because the conversation had taken a distinctly confessional turn? She watched while he went to the fridge and pulled out a bottle of champagne, efficiently disposing of foil and cork before handing her a fizzing glassful.

Sorcha sat up in bed, sipping at the cool champagne while Cesare climbed back in beside her, thinking that she really ought to be enjoying this moment. Imagine if she wrote about it in a postcard home. In bed, over-looking Regent's Park. Fabulous sex. Fabulous man. Fabulous wine.

So why was there this terrible ache of emptiness inside her?

'It wouldn't take very long,' she said.

Cesare frowned as he took a long draught—he who never drank in the middle of the day, but who suddenly wanted something to take the edge off his heightened senses. 'What wouldn't?'

'To list my lovers.'

'I don't want to hear about them, Sorcha,' he clipped out.

'Him.'

His eyes narrowed. 'What?'

'Him, not them. Singular, not plural. Just one. Before you, that is.' She wondered why she was bothering to defend herself—because that was really what it amounted to. Why his opinion should be so important to her. Was it just that she needed him to know that she had acted in an extraordinary way with him—or rather *re*acted? And didn't she run the risk of looking rather pathetic—like someone who was setting out her stall, saying, *Look how relatively untouched I am?*

'One?' he repeated incredulously.

'That surprises you?'

'Of course it does. It isn't many for a woman your age.'

'I didn't realise I was defying some kind of national average.'

'Why did you tell me?' he demanded suddenly.

'Why do you think?' She clutched her glass in two hands in case she spilled wine all over the bed. 'I couldn't bear it if you imagined that I did…well, what I did with you…with lots of men.'

There was a pause, and he knew that in light of her honesty he had to be honest in return. 'I didn't think that, Sorcha,' he said slowly. 'There was such a…' He shrugged. 'That kind of combustive sexual chemistry is rare, believe me—I know.'

He put his glass down, took hers from her hands and placed it beside his, and then drew her into his arms and down onto the bed.

His mouth was cool and tasted of wine, and his body was warm, and Sorcha felt a sudden and overwhelming wave of real yearning which transcended mere sexual desire. She kissed him back, long and deep, and then she rolled out from beneath him, kneeling beside him as she bent her tongue to his nipple.

'Sorcha,' he groaned. 'What do you do to me?'

She let her tongue slide all the way down his belly, along the thin line of hair which arrowed towards where he was hard, and she licked him tentatively, so that he groaned again.

His hands tangled in the silk of her hair as she took him into her mouth, and never had he felt more helpless and vulnerable as she rocked her head up and down. He could feel his climax building and building, and part of him wanted to stop her, to take control away from her and to thrust all that pent-up desire deep into her body.

But it was too late.

She felt the shudder which began to convulse the powerful body, heard an expression of disbelief torn from his lips and closed her eyes as she tasted him. Afterwards he pulled her back up the bed and cradled her in his arms—and that *did* feel like real intimacy.

But she mustn't *do* that—perhaps that was where she went wrong? Thinking that it was more than it was—as if some fantastic orgasm would suddenly give him a complete personality change and he'd start opening his heart to her. But it was in her nature to try, and she wanted him to let her share more than just his body.

She pulled at his shoulder, knowing that it was the wrong thing to do but unable to stop herself. As if she needed to have it written in giant letters for her to finally get the message that he wasn't interested in anything deeper than this.

'Cesare?'

He sighed, knowing just from the tone of her voice what was coming. 'What?'

'Why did you come back?' She met his eyes as he turned back to face her. 'Oh, I know that you're friends with Rupert, and you wanted to do him a favour, and you'll probably make lots of money—but why was it so important for you to seduce me?'

There was silence for a moment.

'Because you were the best sex I never had.' He smiled, but it was a cold and thoughtful smile. 'For years the thought of what I had missed out on ate away at me like a disease, so I wanted to do this—no, I *needed* to— just to lay the ghost of what has haunted me ever since.'

There was a pause. 'I see.' Sorcha let her eyelids close so that he would not detect the wavering hurt which was making her eyes shimmer with tears. 'And now you have.'

But that was the trouble. Cesare narrowed his eyes.

He hadn't.

'We'd better get dressed,' he said abrasively. 'I have a flight to catch.'

'A flight?' she echoed blankly.

'I'm meeting Rupert—we're flying up to the North. The new factory is about to go into production. Remember?'

'Yes, of course.' What an idiot he must think her—they had talked of nothing else for weeks. Yet business couldn't have been further from her mind—all her thoughts were full of *him,* and it was time she pulled herself together. One day soon Cesare would be gone, and she did not need her career to be left in tatters as a consequence of his going.

She stared up at the ceiling. 'It's such a gamble,' she moaned. 'Starting production before you know whether the new campaign will be a success. What if we manufacture loads of extra bottles of sauce and nobody buys them?'

'Life is a gamble, Sorcha—and sometimes you just have to go out on a limb and take a risk.' He stroked his finger over her face. 'I'll only be gone a few days. Will you miss me?'

Sorcha began to get dressed without answering—because what did he expect? Adoring compliments or declarations of affection? How egotistical was that? Especially as he had been so brutally honest about what she meant to *him.*

She bit her lip.

It wasn't the most glowing testament in the world, was it?

She was the best sex he'd never had.

CHAPTER NINE

'THERE'S a journalist outside,' said Rupert. 'And he says he wants to speak to Sorcha.'

All eyes around the table looked at her. The board-room was packed with accountants, operations managers and sales reps, but all Sorcha was aware of was the piercing black gaze which seemed to be stripping her bare—or was that simply wishful thinking on her part? Oh, but she had missed him.

Cesare had been away for weeks. He'd flown straight from the new factory over to the States, and then back to Italy for the centenary celebrations of one of the di Arcangelo department stores. He'd been in regular contact—but you never really knew what was going on behind the scenes when you dealt in phone calls and e-mails.

He had arrived back to discover that a lot of the press interest seemed to be focussed more on the fiery-haired model than on the product—which was every marketing man's idea of a nightmare. He had only calmed down when he had seen the sales figures, which had gone through the roof.

Across the boardroom he met Sorcha's green eyes with soft fire—because even the supremely confident Cesare had been unprepared for the ripple effect of his original idea.

Nobody could have predicted the outrageous success of his revamped advertising campaign. As Rupert had said, products hadn't just been flying off the shelves— they had been leaving them in whole squadrons!

'So, are you going to talk to this journalist, Sorcha?' Cesare questioned, his voice underpinned with silken sarcasm. 'Or perhaps we should think about hiring a PR person especially for you, who could cope with all the interview requests!'

'There's no need to make it sound like something *I've* done, when this whole campaign idea was *your* suggestion,' she retorted. 'If you start rubbishing it now, then it doesn't really reflect well on *your* judgement, does it, Cesare?'

They glared at each other across the room. Had he thought that his absence might bring him immunity from desire? He wanted her, he realised. He still wanted her. He had missed her like crazy. Crazy. His scowl deepened. 'So, are you going to talk to him?'

She looked around the table. 'I'm happy to take advice on it.'

Rupert shrugged. 'Well, you know what they say— there's no such thing as bad publicity.'

'It's certainly been good for Maceo!' piped up one of the secretaries, who had been completely smitten by the Italian photographer.

The campaign had given Maceo's retrospective exhibition an extra boost of publicity. The photos he had taken of Sorcha were absolutely brilliant, causing one of the broadsheet newspapers to wonder why he had given up taking photos professionally.

'I don't know what all the fuss is about,' said Sorcha, wishing that some of it might die down.

'Are you being disingenuous?' Cesare's voice was withering as his gaze flickered over the giant poster of Sorcha sucking on a digit. 'It looks like soft porn!'

'Thanks!' she snapped. 'I can't believe you just said that. *You* approved the original concept—remember?'

'I was not expecting it to look like…like…!' But that was not strictly true. He had known exactly what it would look like. He had underestimated the interest it would provoke, true—and he had also failed to take into account the fact that he would still be feeling this frustrating and pointless jealousy. Because none of this was working out as he had wanted.

He had planned to have cast her aside by now—instead of which, he had flown back hungry for more of her. And—damn it—he didn't *want* to want her—not any more! Looking for something to focus his rage on, he looked again at the poster. 'What was Maceo thinking of?'

'Sales, presumably,' she said sarcastically.

Now they faced one another.

'The journalist is waiting, Sorcha,' Rupert reminded her quietly.

Part of her wanted to go out and do an interview just to rile Cesare. But she knew that wouldn't be the act of a mature person, and so she shook her head. 'Well, I don't want to talk to anyone. Rupes, would you mind referring them to our PR people? Say that my contribution to the campaign was a one-off and that I shan't be doing any more photo-shoots?'

Rupert pulled a face. 'Crikey—are you sure, sis? Don't you want to capitalise on this?'

'There's nothing *to* capitalise on.' Sorcha met the mockery in Cesare's eyes and hesitated. She wanted to say how much she had given up to go to college—but wouldn't that be a revelation too far, especially now, here, in front of all these people? And especially in front of *him.* But there were other ways of saying that her education had been both important and necessary to her.

'I didn't work hard at university to see my entire career culminating in being the face on the front of a sauce bottle.'

Black eyes burned into her.

'Yeah,' said Rupert, nodding. 'And we kept that other photo for over fifty years—so there's probably no need!'

'Rupert!' said Sorcha indignantly. 'That wasn't why I said it! It's a bit much to have my magnanimous gesture thrown back in my face!'

But to her astonishment everyone started clapping,

and even Cesare was giving a grim kind of smile—and, oh, *why* should that feel like a far greater achievement than quadrupling sales?

Because she had missed him like mad, in spite of all the things he'd said to her in bed that afternoon in the hotel? Because she couldn't sleep at nights for thinking about him and he was still obsessing her waking hours, no matter how much she tried?

Had she thought that he might come in here this morning and brush her lips with his when there was a quiet moment, murmur that he'd like to see her alone in his office? And what would she have said? Well, yes, obviously.

But she couldn't have been more wrong.

He hadn't made a single indication that he still wanted her. Not one. No accidental brushing against her arm. No manoeuvring to get them alone together. Nothing. Had he decided while he'd been away that it was better if the affair ended?

'Well, I think that's everything,' Cesare was saying. 'Enjoy Berlin, Rupert.' He looked up as Sorcha stood up. 'Would you mind staying behind for a moment, Sorcha?'

Her heart slammed against her ribcage and a wave of dizziness swept over her. 'Of course.' She waited until everyone had trooped out of the room and looked at him expectantly, wondering if her face hid her terrible fear that it was all over. 'What is it?'

'No ideas about what might be on my mind?'

She was about to say, *I'm not really in the mood for*

riddles, when something in his eyes stopped her. 'This is a…well, it's a bizarre situation, isn't it? You coming back after everything that's—'

He cut across her words with a ruthless statement. 'You still want me.'

It was not a question.

There was a pause as she looked at him.

'Yes.'

'And yet you do not take the initiative?' He walked over to the window and leaned against it, his legs slightly apart, hands resting on his narrow hips. 'You do not ring me while I am away, or send me a text. Or even come into work early this morning, knowing that I am back.' *Waiting for you.*

His lips curved into a mocking smile. 'What's the matter, Sorcha? For all your professed love of equality and independence are you really one of those little-girl lovers who have to be seduced? Perhaps to absolve them from any guilt that they might feel?' His black eyes glittered. 'So that if a man starts to kiss them and touch them they feign a little resistance—and when they can resist no more and give in… Well.' He shrugged his shoulders. 'Then they have no one to blame but the man.'

'Who's talking about blame?' Sorcha shifted uncomfortably. 'Not me.'

'So how long are we going to keep up this ridiculous charade of pretending that we don't want something when we're dying to give in to it? You want me, Sorcha.

So why the hell don't you come over here and have me, before time runs out?'

'Before time runs out?' she echoed. 'What do you mean?'

He laughed. 'Are you crazy? Do you think that I'm going to carry on staying at that…*hotel,* keeping an eye on your little company, when I have plenty of my own to run? Do you think I'm here for keeps—to be your lover whenever the whim takes you?'

Sorcha winced. It was funny the games that your mind could play on you. She had always known he would go, and yet some part of her had imagined him staying here, frozen in some kind of time warp, until some kind of resolution had been made. Except that there wasn't going to be a resolution. They were just two very different people who happened to be overwhelmingly attracted to each other.

The best sex he'd never had.

For Sorcha it was different, because she had grown to realise that Cesare meant more to her than that. He always had done. The love she had felt at eighteen had been real enough, but as fragile and as tender as her age. He had frightened her then, with his lack of emotion, and that was why she had hit out blindly and rejected him. Deep-down she had known that it had been the right thing to do—but hadn't she always regretted that it had ended the way it had?

She knew that she had wounded his pride, and maybe he would never forgive her for that, and yet she wanted to get closer to him and didn't know if that was possible. No one was saying they could go back—but couldn't they build on the huge and obvious attraction between them? Didn't men relax their guard when they had sex with a woman? Even a man as formidable as Cesare?

And now he had told her that his time here was limited—it was down to that old thing of choice again. Should she live for the moment and remain his lover? Or should she opt for her own kind of pride and withdraw gracefully while she still had the opportunity to do so?

She turned her back on him and Cesare felt the sharp tang of disappointment. But he would get over it. There was no way he was going to beg. Until he saw her walk over to the door and lock it, and then come back towards him, unbuttoning her blouse as she did so.

His eyes narrowed in question. 'Sorcha?' He swallowed with difficulty.

'What?' The final button freed, she took the blouse off and hung it carefully over the back of a chair. 'Can't have it creased for my meeting this afternoon, now, can I?' she questioned innocently.

'Sorcha—'

He made to move, but she stayed him exactly where he was with an imperious gesture. Her hand reached round to unclip her skirt and then to slide the zip down. She stepped out of it, folded it, and hung it next to the blouse.

She turned to face him wearing nothing but a lacy bra, panties, silk stockings and a suspender belt. And high heels. Cesare swallowed. Oh, those heels! Briefly, he closed his eyes.

'Have you missed me?' she questioned.

'Yes.'

'Then come away from the window,' she told him, 'and show me how much.'

For a moment he honestly wasn't sure whether he could move, but somehow he managed it. Loosening his tie, he began walking towards her, and something in his eyes made hers widen.

'Cesare?' she questioned uncertainly.

He gave a low laugh. 'What's the matter, Sorcha?' he murmured as he stood in front of her. 'Bitten off more than you can *chew*?' And he took her unprotesting hand and ran it along the hard ridge of his erection, shuddering as he did so.

'Feel in my back pocket,' he suggested silkily.

She did, kneading his buttock as she extracted a condom. 'Do you always come prepared?' she questioned unsteadily.

'I don't always come,' he murmured, wryly remembering their first rather one-sided encounter on the boardroom table.

'Then I'd better make sure you do today,' she whispered.

'Oh, Sorcha.'

The way he said her name made her want to dissolve. She wanted to kiss him—tiny, tender kisses on every centimetre of his silky olive skin—but she suspected that kissing wasn't part of this erotic scene they seemed to be making up as they went along. And kissing made her weak—whereas seduction was giving her power.

She undid his belt and unzipped him, carefully freed him—easing him out into the palm of her hand—and he moaned.

'Shhh. I don't want anyone to know what we're doing.'

He found the fact that she had told him to be quiet unbearably erotic—almost as erotic as her kicking off her own tiny panties, pushing him down to the floor and then straddling him.

'How's *that?*' she questioned disingenuously as she lowered herself down to sheath his silken steel column.

He shook his head, unable to speak, unable to do anything except helplessly lie there while she rode him. Oh, sweet heaven…

He began to cry out as sweet release seized him, and she lowered her head to capture his mouth, her lace-covered breasts covering him with their warm curves as she kissed him. And still she thrust her hips towards him, so that as his pleasure began to fade out her own orgasm swept her away, and she arched her body like a bow.

He caught her bottom and anchored himself to it, watching as she threw her head back and moaned—silky hair tumbling all the way down her back.

When it was over, they stayed exactly where they were—controlling their unsteady breathing, staring at one another in quiet disbelief.

'What's Italian for "wow!"?' mumbled Sorcha.

'It's the same.' He stroked his hand over her waist reflectively, and then lifted his arm to glance at his watch. 'Better move, baby,' he murmured, with the lightest of smacks on her bottom. 'I have a phone call to make.'

'Sure.' Somehow Sorcha kept her face composed, even if his words made her feel like a discarded hooker.

But you shouldn't start a no-strings office affair unless you could accept it for what it was.

Sex.

CHAPTER TEN

'How about some coffee?'

Cesare looked up from the paperwork he'd been working his way through at his desk, and his eyes narrowed as they focussed on Sorcha.

'What?' he questioned, and rubbed at his temples.

'Coffee,' said Sorcha, wondering why she couldn't get rid of the feeling that she just wanted to shake this whole situation to make it the same as it had been before he'd left for his long trip to the new factory, the States and Italy. But she couldn't. And it wasn't.

In the bittersweet days since he'd returned Sorcha thought he'd been distancing himself from her—despite the red-hot satisfaction of their sex-life. Was it just a kind of preparation for his eventual departure? Or was it just her paranoia?

Cesare stifled a yawn. He had worked late last night, after everyone else had gone home, and then done a conference call with LA. And since he'd arrived that morning he'd been ploughing through a pile of papers with Sorcha on the other side of the table until she had disappeared into the private cloakroom a few minutes ago.

Now she had reappeared, and it seemed that she had taken off her shoes and stockings. Cesare saw the glint in her shimmering green eyes and guessed from their hungry expression and from the way she was walking that her panties must have come off too.

She wasn't just offering him coffee, that was for sure.

'I'd love some,' he replied blandly.

Sorcha frowned. 'Coffee?'

He leaned back in his chair and studied her, rubbing his eyes. 'That *was* what you were offering me, *cara*—unless my ears were mistaken.'

Giving him a slightly unsure smile, Sorcha dropped her shoes onto the carpet and walked over to the coffee machine, where she fiddled around and poured two espressos, then put them both on his desk.

'Here you are.'

'Thanks.'

She watched him pick his up and sip it, and frowned. She had thought that he might have telephoned her last night when he'd finished working. She had been willing to slip over to the hotel to see him—but he hadn't phoned.

And she had deliberately arrived at the office early this morning—but he had sauntered in after Rupert, and there had been back-to-back meetings all day. All she'd been able to do was look at him with a kind of helpless longing and growing frustration.

She felt as if she was doing a balancing act the

whole time—trying to appear cool and not look as if she was some desperado whose world was going to cave in after he'd gone.

But even she had her limits—and surely, as his lover, a few rights, too? She drew a deep breath. 'So, are you going to tell me what's wrong?'

'Wrong?' Cesare put his cup down, and now Sorcha could see the shadows beneath his eyes and a pang of guilt suddenly hit her. 'Why should anything be wrong?'

'I just thought…' Her words tailed off as she read something in his eyes she didn't recognise.

He stood up and came towards her.

'What?' he demanded. 'You thought that something might be wrong because for once I didn't leap up and start tearing at your clothes when you snapped your pretty little fingers?'

'But I thought that's what you like to do!' Sorcha stared at him. 'You've never complained before.'

'Of course I haven't!' he said, in a voice of dangerous silk. 'Because what man in his right mind would complain when a woman is constantly demanding mind-blowing, erotic, no-strings sex and demanding that *he* keep it secret?'

'Presumably you have your reasons,' she said coolly.

Cesare stared at her in frustration. It was the fantasy that most men dreamed of—and he was fulfilling every sweet, sensational second of it.

He had tried telling Maceo about it over dinner in Rome last week, and the photographer had told him that if he was really complaining he needed to see a psychi-atrist, because no-strings relationships were the only ones which worked—and did he think Sorcha might be interested in doing more modelling? Cesare had swal-lowed a mouthful of wine and told his friend to go to hell.

Cesare studied Sorcha thoughtfully. 'We never spend the whole night together—never sleep together,' he observed.

'That might be a bit of a giveaway, don't you think?' she asked. 'Some bright spark like my mother or my brother might put two and two together and very cleverly come up with the answer of four!'

Cesare knitted his dark brows together. *Maledica la donna!* 'And we never eat together,' he observed.

'That's not true,' she protested. 'We often have a working lunch.'

Sure they did. Tongue sandwiches in a deserted lay-by.

'*And* we had dinner with my family on Sunday—you know we did!'

'Yes, I know that,' he agreed dangerously. 'And when we weren't being forced to endure a hundred damned wedding photos which all looked the same—you spent the whole time studiously avoiding looking at me except when was absolutely necessary. I will tell you some-thing, Sorcha—if anything is designed to alert them to the fact we're having an affair, then that certainly is!'

'Since when did you become such an expert in human behaviour?' she demanded.

He stared at her. 'Since I started dating— *Dating?*'

He gave a hollow laugh. 'Let me rephrase that—since I started having sex with a woman who thinks no further than the nearest erogenous zone!'

She rushed at him with her clenched hand raised to pummel him in the chest, but he caught her easily by the wrist and brought her up close to him.

He could see her eyes dilating so that the green was almost completely obscured by ebony saucers of desire. And he could feel her breath warm against his skin— her lips so close that he could almost taste their sweetness. And how easy it would be. How ridiculously easy.

'Oh, yes,' he taunted. 'You want me now, don't you, Sorcha? You want me right now.'

'You know I always want you,' she answered in confusion. 'Did you…did you start the row deliberately to….?' But she saw the expression of contempt in his eyes and knew that her assessment had gone horribly, horribly wrong.

'You think I wanted to inject a frisson of imaginary *conflict* into our relationship?' he demanded incredulously, and he let her hand fall from his as if it was something contaminated. 'Dear God!'

He walked away from her—away from her sweet allure and her dangerous kind of magic. He looked out of the window at the summer clouds blowing across the sky.

'My wild little Sorcha, who is always up for sexual adventure,' he murmured. 'Anyway, anywhere and anyhow. God forbid that we should just go home to bed at the end of the evening, like any other couple!'

Incredulously, she stared at the formidable set of his back. 'Is that what you want?'

He turned again and his face was expressionless. 'It is too late for that, Sorcha—don't you understand?'

She shook her head, as if trying to dispel the confusion. 'No, I don't understand!'

He shrugged. 'We have forged the pattern of our relationship. It is what it is. We work and we have sex—and now that the work is coming to an end…well, it follows that the sex will, too.'

There was silence.

'Is that all it's been?' she questioned painfully. 'Sex?'

'How would you describe it, then?' he challenged softly.

And suddenly she realised what he was doing. 'Why are you turning this around on me?' she demanded, acknowledging how clever he was. Emotionally, he had pushed her away and sought refuge in sex, and now he was accusing *her* of compartmentalising! She couldn't win, she thought—or rather Cesare didn't want her to. There would be only one winner in this scenario, and he was going to make sure it was him.

'You're the man who runs a million miles away from feelings!' she stormed. 'If I've acted this way, it's only because that's the way you intimated I *should* act. What's the matter, Cesare—are you angry because I've actually gone along with it?'

'That is *enough*!' he gritted.

'No, it isn't! We never talk about the things which are going on inside, do we? Like we never talk about when you asked me to marry you—'

'I don't want to discuss it, Sorcha!' His voice cracked out like a whip.

'Well, I do! You wouldn't listen to me when I tried to explain myself, to tell you that you were frightening me with your list of suitable qualities you desired in a wife. I was eighteen years old, for God's sake, Cesare, and I really loved you. All I wanted was some love and affection in return—and you couldn't give it to me.'

She waited, wanting some reaction, some denial, or even a furious justification—but there was nothing. His face was like ice, his expression frozen, and Sorcha let out a shuddering breath. Nothing had changed, not really. Back then he hadn't been listening, and he wasn't listening now.

'I'm sorry,' she whispered, because she saw now that she had been wasting her time in ever thinking that they could build something new on the rocky foundations of the past.

'Sorry?' He was angry. How dared she do this to him? Why *should* he subject himself to unnecessary emotional pain, when it was easier just to lose himself in the silken-soft sweetness of her body? And, oh, when he was far away from England he would find himself another woman—one who wouldn't torture him like Sorcha did with all this *stuff*.

He gave a cool smile—which concealed the decision

being made—and he felt a familiar sense of liberation from having made it.

'Cesare?' she whispered tentatively.

'Lock the door,' he ordered.

Sorcha did as he asked, but something was different—or rather, *he* was different. He drew down the blinds and shut the world out so that the light in the office was muted and it was as if they had created their own private world.

And then he took complete control—as if he was giving her a masterclass in seduction. The Latin lover personified, he skimmed his fingertips over her skin, lowering his head to graze his lips over her neck, carrying her over to the leather couch at the far end of the room and laying her down on it.

Her bright hair was tumbled all over her flushed face and he reached down to brush a wayward lock away. Sorcha's eyes suddenly shot open, for something had *changed* and she couldn't work out what it was.

'Cesare?' she whispered again

'Shhh.'

He kissed the tip of her nose, then her eyelids, and then her lips, and it was easy to let her misgivings melt away beneath the expert skill of his touch. She shut her eyes tight as he stroked her and murmured soft words in his native tongue into her ear, and she had to bite back her own desire to tell him how much she—

Her eyes snapped open as he entered her, and he stilled.

'What is it?'

Sorcha swallowed. 'Nothing,' she whispered. She tangled her fingers in his thick dark hair as he moved again, and the sweetness of the act was enough to push crazy and stupid thoughts out of her head.

I don't love you, she thought brokenly. *I don't want to love you.*

Afterwards, they lay there, with Sorcha struggling to get her thoughts back on some kind of normal track, but she felt as if she were trying to wade through treacle as she battled to tell the difference between what was real and what was fantasy.

You don't love him.

He lifted her off him and began pulling on his clothes again. 'I'm catching a flight to Rome this evening,' he said.

'But you've only been back a few days!'

'I need to have one last look at those figures. And get a few things straight in my mind.' He gave a brisk, slightly efficient smile—she had seen him use it with the secretaries, but never with her. *Never with her.*

'The company is doing just fine,' he continued. 'The new factory is up and running—in fact, the relaunch has succeeded beyond my wildest dreams.'

He spoke in the gentle tone of a doctor who was delivering a horrendous prognosis to a patient—a mixture of kindness and resignation. She wanted to grab hold of his broad, strong shoulders and yell, *I don't care about the company—what about us?*

But something in his eyes stopped her. Was it a warning? That they could do this in one of two ways—

and if they chose the dignified way to end it, then they needed the assistance of their old friend.

Pride.

'You're leaving, aren't you, Cesare?' she questioned, using every effort of will to prevent her voice from breaking.

'You knew I had to leave some time.'

Of course she had. 'And…what will you do?'

'I'll go home to Panicale. I don't want to miss the harvest this year.'

Something in the way he said it made her heart heavy. Her lips framed the question she hardly dared ask, and yet some masochistic urge compelled her to. 'You sound like a man who has a yearning to settle down.'

'Well, of course I do, Sorcha—doesn't everyone? One day I want a family of my own, as I imagine you do, too.'

She saw a glimpse of his future and saw that she had no place in it. So this really was the end. Sorcha swallowed down an impending sense of terrible loss.

She thought about the tips Maceo had given her when he'd been taking her photo. That if you pretended you felt something hard enough, then it would look real to the outside world. And if that was what Cesare really thought of her, then railing against it wasn't going to change his mind.

'What time's your flight?' she asked.

Cesare's face did not betray one flicker of reaction, and indeed he convinced himself that the brief twist of his heart was merely surprise at her response. Why, he

'Well, you're the one who booked it!'

'Please don't remind me!'

Sorcha stared at the jammed road ahead, and sighed. 'Why don't you tell me how you know the photographer?' she said.

'Are you trying to change the subject?'

'What do you think?'

There was a silence.

'Well?' she prompted.

It was hardly a state secret, was it? 'Maceo and I have known each other since we were kids,' he said.

'Schoolfriends, you mean?'

Cesare's mouth twisted. 'Not exactly.'

'Not exactly…what? Neighbours?'

'No. We met at judo lessons.'

'And you've been friends ever since?'

'Men don't look at friendship in the same way as women,' he answered slowly. 'But, yes, we're friends. Look, we're here,' he murmured, unable to hide his relief as they drew up outside the studio. 'You go inside. I'll see you in a while.'

Sorcha turned to look at him. 'Lucky me,' she said, and his eyes glittered in response.

'That's exactly what you said last night,' he murmured. 'Twice, I recall.'

'Only twice?' she retorted, and he laughed.

The assistant's voice broke into her erotic thoughts. 'Don't bite your lip, Sorcha—there's a good girl!'

should applaud her poise and her cool control. How many times had he told a lover that he was leaving only to have her sobbing and begging and pleading with him not to go, or to take her with him?

His mouth curved into a mocking smile. For once, he had met his match—and the irony was that what made them so alike was the very thing which would ensure they had no future together.

'At eight.' He lifted his arm to glance at his watch. 'I want to go and say goodbye to the staff at the factory.'

'Do you...?' She gave him a tentative smile, but she wasn't going to put him in the awkward position of having to reject her. She injected her question with just the right amount of levity. 'Do you want me to come and do the waving hankie thing?'

It occurred to Cesare that Sorcha Whittaker really must be his nemesis if she could make such a flippant comment when he was walking out of her life for good. Did he really mean so little to her that her beautiful mouth could curve into that cool and unfeeling smile? Damn her...*damn* her!

He hadn't intended this, but he knew that he had to do it one last time. Reaching for her, he snaked his arm round her waist and very deliberately brought her up close, so that she could feel the hot, hard heat of his new erection, and he saw her pupils dilate with surprise and pleasure.

'No need for that,' he murmured. He unzipped himself and sheathed himself in protection for one last time. 'Because when I remember you, I want to re-member you just like…*this.*'

Sorcha was glad that he entered her with that great powerful thrust, and glad when he began to move inside her, so that she could pretend her stifled cry was one of pleasure rather than pain.

Maybe it was better this way.

CHAPTER ELEVEN

'IS SOMETHING the matter, dear?'

Sorcha put the post down on the breakfast table and looked at her mother with a smile which felt as heavy as her heart. 'Wrong? No, of course not. Why should there be?'

Virginia Whittaker poured Earl Grey tea into bone-china cups and added a sliver of lemon. 'You just seem a little…out of sorts?' she observed delicately.

One sure-fire way of getting over something was not keeping it alive by talking about it, so Sorcha took the cup of tea with a bland smile.

'Oh, it's probably all the excitement of my short-lived career as a sauce bottle model,' she said airily.

'And nothing to do with the fact that Cesare di Arcangelo has gone back, I suppose?' questioned her mother shrewdly.

Just the mention of his name brought his dark, mocking face back into her mind with heartbreaking clarity, and yet their farewell seemed to mock her with its cold lack of passion. Two cool kisses on either cheek, followed by an equally cool look in his black eyes.

He had climbed into his sports car with all his stuff— including the brand-new silver beer tankard with his name inscribed on it, which everyone in the factory had clubbed together for and presented to him.

'Cesare's been very popular with the workforce,' Rupert had confided.

Sorcha had ached, and hearing things like that hadn't helped. The fact that everyone else thought Cesare was Mr Wonderful made her wonder what she had done wrong. She felt as if she had missed out—as if she had played it all wrong with Cesare. Except that relationships weren't supposed to be a game, were they?

And added to her sense of loss was the certainty that the factory was too small for more than one boss. This was Rupert's niche, not hers—and now it was too full of memories of Cesare for her to ever be able to settle. She certainly couldn't carry on living at home like this, but her flat was let out for the whole year. They had offered her a post in the new factory, but she didn't want to uproot herself and go and live in a part of the country where she knew no one—because that would surely only increase her isolation.

Her mother's voice broke into Sorcha's thoughts. 'And I suppose you must be missing your affair with him?'

The bone-china cup very nearly met an untimely end, and Sorcha put it down with a hand which was trembling.

'You…you *knew?* You knew I was having an affair with Cesare?'

Virginia sighed. 'Oh, Sorcha—of *course* I knew. Everyone knew. It was as obvious as the nose on your face—even though you did everything you could to try to hide it.'

So all that effort had been for nothing! Her attempts to make it seem as if it were not happening had been totally transparent—and in so doing she had lost the opportunity to spend a whole night with him.

'Maybe I'm not such a good liar as I thought I was,' she said, swallowing down the sudden salty taste of tears which tainted her mouth.

'Are you in love with him?'

'No.'

'I agree, Sorcha,' said her mother wryly. 'You're actually a hopeless liar.'

'Mum, I'm *not* in love with him. I'm… It's…*complicated.*' She sighed. 'We've got history and, yes, we're hugely attracted—but he wants the kind of woman who's docile and will fit in with whatever he wants, while I'm…'

Her voice tailed off. Just what *was* she? And what did *she* want? The things which had once seemed so important to her now seemed to have lost their impact. As if she had been seeing the world in a certain way and it had suddenly blurred and changed its focus without her realising it.

'I'm an independent woman,' she finished, with a touch of defiance. Someone who neither wanted nor needed anyone else—yet look what had happened, no matter how much she tried to deny it. She both wanted and needed a man who did not reciprocate her feelings.

Her mother sliced through a ripe peach. 'Has he been in touch?'

Sorcha shook her head. 'He phoned Rupert after he told him about the small business award we've been nominated for.'

'Well, that's good news, isn't it, darling?'

'I suppose so.'

'And even if things haven't worked out with Cesare there are plenty of other men. I can't tell you how many people have been coming up to me in the village and saying how it brightens their day when they pick up their sauce and shake you all over their omelette!'

Great, thought Sorcha. Nice way to be remembered.

Naturally, being nominated for a small business award was good publicity, and Sorcha was pleased for the company—and even more pleased to see how happy Rupert was.

'Cesare gave me the confidence to believe in myself and the business,' he had said quietly. 'And now I do.'

Bully for Cesare, thought Sorcha sourly.

She went through the mechanics of living—presenting to the world a close approximation of what Sorcha Whittaker was like. But inside it was like having something gnawing away at her and leaving a great, gaping hole. Had she once wondered if it was possible to feel as deeply as she had done as a teenager? Now she knew the answer certainly to be yes—but what she had not banked on was the level of pain, the aching deep inside her that she couldn't seem to fill with anything.

And then an invitation dropped through the letterbox—a stiff cream card, heavily embossed with gold, inviting Sorcha to a retrospective of Maceo di Ciccio's work in a prestigious gallery situated on the Thames in London.

'Are you going?' asked Emma, who was almost unbearable to be with—her 'loved-upness' so tangible that it seemed to be emanating from her in waves, even all these weeks after her honeymoon.

'I haven't decided.'

'Oh, do *go,* Sorcha—he might have included a photo of you, in your famous gingham apron!'

'Very funny.'

'And anyway,' Emma added mischievously, 'Cesare might be there.'

'Oh, *do* shut up,' said Sorcha crossly.

But he *might* be, mightn't he?

Was that why Sorcha took such inordinate care about her appearance—even going to the rather devious lengths of wearing a floaty skirt.

Just so he can put his hand up it? mocked the voice of her conscience and she drew herself up short—because, yes, that was the truth of it. Cesare liked women wearing skirts and dresses—he had said so—and here she was, conforming to his idea of what a woman should be. Wasn't that disgraceful?

But she didn't change. Instead she drove into London

with a fast-beating heart, and had to park miles away from her eventual destination.

It was a windy day, and the river was all silver as a pale, ineffectual sun struggled to make itself seen.

The gallery was beautiful—vast, with huge windows, and lit with the double dose of light which bounced off the restless water.

There were photos from every phase of Maceo's development as a photographer. Moody black and white shots of the backstreets of a city she took to be Rome, and countless pictures of the world's most beautiful women. He was good, thought Sorcha wryly.

In fact, he was more than good, she thought as she came across some of the tougher themes he'd handled: war and famine, natural and man-made disasters— photos which made you want to rail at the injustices in life.

And then—nerve-rackingly and unexpectedly—she came across a photo of herself. It was not, as Emma had teased, an advertising shot taken in the ghastly gingham apron, but a close-up taken when she hadn't realised that the camera had been trained on her.

She had been looking up, a look of consternation on her face, her eyes big and lost—as if something had just been wrenched away from her. And she knew just when it had been taken. When she had heard the door slam. When Cesare had jealously stormed out of the studio because Maceo had been getting her to pout and flirt outrageously.

She stared at the picture she made—a picture of longing and uncertainty, of a woman who was on the brink of falling in love again. But Cesare would not have seen that. He would only have caught the split-second before, when her face had assumed a seductive mask to sell a product. Yet here she was without the mask—and, oh, Maceo had managed to penetrate right through to the raw emotions beneath. Cesare was right—his friend had a real talent for seeing what was really there.

'Do you like it?' asked a velvety voice at her side, and Sorcha turned her head to see Maceo standing there, studying his own photo intently and then turning his head to look at her with his hard, brilliant eyes.

'It's…'

'Revealing?' he murmured.

'Possibly.'

She thought how edgy he seemed today, in his trademark black, with none of the flamboyant behaviour he'd displayed in the studio. Or was that because she no longer had the protective presence of Cesare in the background?

Suddenly she felt a little out of place. It struck Sorcha that Maceo had his own mask which he donned whenever he needed to. Everyone did. She just wondered what lay behind Cesare's. She looked around. Was there the slightest chance that he *might* be here?

Maceo raised his dark brows. 'Have you seen him?' he asked coolly.

If it had been anyone else she might have said, Who?—but it wasn't just Maceo's camera lens which stripped away the artifice, Sorcha realised, as those black eyes pierced through her.

'You mean he's here?' she questioned, her heart leaping with painful hope in her breast.

His mouth curved into an odd kind of smile. 'No. He isn't here. I meant his photo.'

Sorcha shook her head. 'No. No, I haven't.'

His eyes had narrowed and he seemed to be subjecting her to some kind of silent assessment. 'Come with me,' he said softly.

Sorcha followed him across the silent polished floor of the gallery, aware from the glances and the little buzz of the spectators that he had been recognised, but a small phalanx of assistants walking at a discreet distance kept any fans at bay.

He took her into a room that she hadn't noticed, a smaller one, with family photos—obviously his—and Sorcha had to bite back a gasp as she saw the terrible poverty in which he had grown up.

And then her gaze alighted on a group shot of some teenage boys in singlets and jeans, all with their arms folded, gazing with suspicion at the camera.

She saw Cesare immediately—to her prejudiced eye he looked the fittest and the strongest, and of course the most stunningly handsome of the lot. But how young he looked—extraordinarily young. And something else, too...

'How old was he when this was taken?' she questioned slowly.

'Eighteen.'

Eighteen. The age *she* had been that summer, when he had come to the house, when she'd felt so mixed and jumbled up inside, so frightened of the future and all the consequences of her choices.

Yet here on Cesare's face was the similar uncertainty of youth—the sense of standing on a precipice and not knowing whether you should step back to safety or take that leap of faith into the unknown. Had she imagined that he had never known a moment's uncertainty or doubt—even as a teenager?

Yes, of course she had. When she had met him he had been in his mid-twenties—polished and sexy and supremely confident. But that was just the external packaging.

What lay beneath?

When she'd turned down Cesare's proposal of marriage she had known that his pride had been wounded—but what about his heart? She hadn't even considered that, because she had only thought about how *she* felt. Why had she never credited him with having feelings like she did—of pain and hurt and fear of loneliness?

Just because he behaved in a shuttered way and didn't show his emotions, it didn't mean he didn't *have* them, did it? Why, she had never even stopped for a moment to wonder just *why* he behaved that way. She had never dared try to explore the substance of the man under the brilliant patina of charisma and success.

She had never allowed herself to consider that there was a chance that somehow they *could* be happy. And would she ever forgive herself if she didn't find out?

She stared at the photo of the teenage boy, knowing that she had to be willing to put her feelings on the line and run the risk that she might be rejected. The risk which Cesare had talked of didn't just apply to businesses, but to relationships, too. It was part of life. But this time a rejection would be final. A clean break. A sharp and terrible hurt, but one from which she could allow herself to heal properly and rid herself at last of the terrible ache of regret.

She turned to the photographer. 'Thanks, Maceo,' she said, a little shakily.

He shrugged. *'Ciao, bella,'* he said coolly.

He doesn't approve of me, thought Sorcha suddenly, and wondered what it was she was supposed to have done. But she wasn't going to let Maceo's opinion of her distract her from what she knew she had to do.

She rang the airline from her mobile and learned that there was a flight to Rome later that afternoon. Grateful to a college lecturer who had once told her to always carry her passport with her 'just in case', she booked it. Well, why not? she asked herself. What was the point in delaying?

She drove to Heathrow and parked, and there was time before the flight to buy some underwear, toiletries and a phrasebook—it wasn't until she was mid-air that Sorcha began to realise that this was pretty rash. But it felt better just *doing* something instead of moping around at home. Regrets were terrible things. They ate away at you and eroded your chances of finding peace and contentment.

But by the time she found a delighted taxi driver who was willing to take her out to Panicale, she was seriously beginning to question the wisdom of her actions.

Was she mad?

The motorway cut through huge patchwork mountains where toffee-coloured cows grazed and fields of sunflowers became more muted as the sun set and nighttime began to fall.

The driver was obviously labouring under the illusion that his cab was a sports car, and Sorcha tried to distract herself by staring out at the cloudy sky and wondering if she should have phoned Cesare to tell him she was on her way.

No.

She needed to see his face, his first instinctive reaction to her. Some heated things had been said in their conversation before he'd left—words which he might or might not have meant—just like some of the things she'd said.

And how was she going to explain her sudden bizarre appearance? She would be guided by him—if he scooped her up into his arms and told her that there hadn't been a moment when he'd stopped thinking about her...

She leaned back in the seat and closed her eyes. Oh,

please. They would hold each other tight, and she would have to show him that she *did* have a heart that loved and yearned and beat like a drum only for him.

And if he didn't?

That was the risk she ran—and anyway, it was too late to back out now, because the car was squeezing through a narrow stone arch over a track which seemed to bump upwards for ages. But there were the lights of habitation in the distance, and Sorcha's heart was in her mouth as the cab drew to a halt.

'Quanto e esso, per favore?' she asked.

The driver gave her a price, and it was expensive—but then the journey had taken close to two hours.

Sorcha remembered the other word she had learned on the plane. *'Per favore…attesa?'* Because she needed him to wait in case Cesare wasn't there—or in case the unthinkable happened and he didn't want to see her. Or he was with another woman.

'Si, signorina.'

The air was heavy and close, and Sorcha thought she heard the distant rumble of thunder. Tiny beads of sweat sprang up on her forehead and her hands were literally shaking as she walked across the soft grass towards the villa, where she could make out splashes of light which shone through an abundance of trees.

What was she going to say?

The door was open, and she stepped inside and heard voices and laughter and chatter and, incongruously, a baby crying. Her eyes opened in alarm.

What had she done? For a moment she almost imagined that Cesare had been living some kind of bizarre double life—that he had been conducting an affair with *her* while secretly flying back here to see his wife and child.

But she knew that he would never do that—in her heart she knew that Cesare was a man of principle and integrity, and that such a double betrayal would be alien to his nature.

So did this mean he was having some kind of *party?*

It certainly sounded like it.

She felt like someone in a film as she walked silently along the long corridor towards the sounds of merriment. As if she would find…

What?

The sound was coming from outside, on the far side of the house, and Sorcha walked through a vast kitchen and open-plan dining room to where she could see candles guttering on a table on the terrace.

Ignoring the small shout of consternation from a chef who was swirling flames around in a frying pan, Sorcha stepped onto the terrace to see a table set for dinner and four adults seated around it, plus a small child.

Five faces turned towards her, and the conversation dried up as if some celestial director had muted the sound. Only the child gurgled.

Sorcha barely registered the faces of the others—only distantly noting that one was male and two were female. How neat. How tidy.

Cesare was staring at her with an expression she didn't recognise. There was no smile. No word of welcome. Nothing but the cold glitter of disbelief in his black eyes.

'*Madre di Dio!*' he ground out beneath his breath, and rose to his feet.

CHAPTER TWELVE

CESARE stared at her and felt the great slam of his heart against his ribcage, its sudden powerful pounding as it leapt into life. 'Sorcha?' he demanded. 'What are you doing here?'

It was the greeting from hell—or at least from her very worst nightmare. Keep calm, Sorcha, she told herself as she felt herself sway a little. You have a get-out clause for just this eventuality—remember?

'There's a taxi waiting for me,' she said calmly, as if women just arrived from England at any old time and then turned straight back again. 'I'll…I'll go back to the airport.'

'Don't be so absurd,' said Cesare, but the coolness in his voice remained. 'I will go and dismiss him. Sit down—you look terrible. Luca will pour you some wine. This is Sorcha, everyone.'

He spoke in rapid Italian and the other man immediately stood up to pull out an available chair for her—at the end of the table, naturally, as far from Cesare as it was possible to be.

Sorcha didn't want to sit down. She wanted some giant hand to magic her away from here, from the bemused and frankly unwelcoming expressions of the people around the table. But she was feeling distinctly shaky, and she also recognised that it would look utterly ridiculous if she just disappeared again.

'Here.' Luca pressed a glass of red wine into her hand and Sorcha sipped it gratefully, nodding a kind of greeting at their collective faces, as if trying to resurrect a little bit of social grace in a situation which certainly didn't feature in any etiquette book.

They were all Italian—and why would they be anything else?

One of the women said, 'You have travelled far?'

'From…England, actually.' How bizarre it sounded.

It seemed difficult to follow that, and no one else said a word. They all sat there in an awkward silence and waited for Cesare to return from dismissing the taxi. He seemed to take for ever, but when he did, he was holding aloft a plastic carrier bag which was filled with shampoo, conditioner and knickers. In the darkness, Sorcha blushed.

'Your luggage, I believe?' he drawled, and deposited it by her chair. Then he said something in Italian and some of the frost in the atmosphere seemed to evaporate—but only by a fraction.

He shot her a look. She had taken him by surprise,

and it was not a familiar role for him to be cast in—
especially in front of other people. She was on *his* territory, and she must understand that they did things dif-
ferently here. If she was expecting him to drop
everything and leave the table in order to...what? Why
was she here?

A smile curved his lips. 'My friends were concerned
that you might be some kind of stalker—some disgruntled
ex-girlfriend—but I reassured them that I was unlikely to
offer a glass of wine to anyone who posed a threat.'

She knew that he was trying to salvage a fairly impossible situation, but Sorcha could have curled up and died.
Yet how else must it look to these sophisticated people?

Because sophisticated they certainly were.

'Let me introduce you,' Cesare said wryly. 'Luca
you've met—and this is his wife, Pia, with Gino, my
godson.' His black eyes softened as he glanced at the
toddler, and then his gaze travelled to the other guest—
a woman in black silk, with a blunt-cut raven bob and
shiny lips the colour of claret. 'And this is Letizia...'

How easy it was to notice the absence of a wedding
ring on the woman's finger, the way she looked up at
Cesare and then at Sorcha, the unmistakable body
language which said, *He's already taken!* Sorcha met
her bright, hard dark eyes.

'Hello,' said Sorcha.

'Do you speak Italian, Sorcha?' asked Letizia
guilelessly.

'Unfortunately, no—I don't.'

'Oh, well. Then you will have to suffer our English.' Letizia gave a tinkling little laugh. 'It will be good for us to practise—*si, Cesare?*'

'*Effettivamente,*' Cesare murmured, his gaze capturing Sorcha's as he lanced her with an impenetrable look. 'I'm *fascinated* to know what has prompted this unexpected visit—and at such an extraordinary time.' He glanced over to the doorway, where a chef was standing with his hands on his hips, looking as if he was about to do battle. 'But, like all great chefs, Stephan is a little temperamental—and as he is just about to serve the entrée it will have to wait until afterwards.'

He raised his eyebrows in imperious query, as if daring her to do anything other than sit there and be guided by him. 'Unless it is so urgent that it cannot wait, Sorcha?'

Oh, yes—sure she was going to blurt it all out *now*.

I think I love you, Cesare. I know how stupidly I've acted, and so I've rushed over here to see if our relationship has any future.

The answer was glaring her in the face as clearly as if he'd spelt it out for her. He was having dinner with a cluster of his mates, which may or may not be part of a packed social calendar. But whether it was or it wasn't didn't really matter—far from sitting around the place moping about her, or even thinking about her, Cesare was living his life.

He had moved on.

'No, that's fine,' she said lightly.

It was the worst meal Sorcha had ever had to endure—and because everyone kept forgetting to speak English she felt more and more of an outsider as every second passed.

But she pushed the food around her plate and tried to keep smiling. At least she was opposite Gino—who was the sweetest little thing and the most amenable of all the guests.

Cesare sipped his wine thoughtfully and stared down the table as she poked a fork uninterestedly at a piece of lettuce. He had never seen her so…

He shook his head. *Why was she here?* Did she have business in this part of Italy? No, of course she didn't. He had heard of travelling light—but three pairs of lacy panties and a toothbrush?

His mouth hardened. Had she decided on a whim that she wanted him? Was that why she had turned up out of the blue like this? Had she been hoping to find him alone and act out some wild sexual fantasy of walking in and pretending that he was a stranger and making hot, silent love to him?

Meeting the burning look of censure in his eyes, Sorcha quickly looked down at her plate. How could she have had the temerity to turn up here like this and try to convince him that in the space of a few days she had undergone a massive change? That she had suddenly discovered she wanted to jack in her supposedly precious career and settle down to a life of cosy domesticity *with him?* Or at least to work out some kind of mid-way compromise. As if he even cared!

Because he hadn't fulfilled his part in her fantasy. *He hadn't asked her to.* He hadn't been sitting, waiting to fling his arms around her and lift her up into the air, to whirl her round and tell her that he loved her and had missed her.

That was only make-believe.

The reality was that he was sitting, laughing and joking with his friends, and it was like seeing a different side of him. In England he had been her powerful and autocratic lover, yes, but never a permanent fixture in her life—he had just dipped in and out of it as mood and circumstance took him. The dark, enigmatic foreigner who always seemed to stand out like an elusive rare breed.

Whereas here he seemed to have become real—it was as if she was watching a black and white photo suddenly begin to glow with glorious colour.

'You are staying long, Sorcha?' asked Letizia suddenly.

'I…' Sorcha glanced up at Cesare, sending out a silent appeal that he come to her rescue, but his black eyes remained flinty and obdurate. 'No,' she finished.

An awkward silence fell over the table, broken only by a distant low rumble of thunder.

Letizia had succeeded in making her feel like the kind of desperado who would stoop to any means to ensnare a captivating and eligible bachelor like Cesare. The kind of woman who would jump on a plane and turn up announced.

They said that eavesdroppers never heard any good

about themselves—well, maybe gatecrashers fared no better. For all she knew, he might have been planning to spend the night with Letizia.

Her face paled as she realised that she was trapped. She had let the taxi go. Beneath the table, her fingers gripped convulsively at the heavy linen napkin. Surely Cesare would not be so insensitive as to put her in one of the spare rooms while he took the luscious Letizia off to his own to spend the night making love to her?

But why shouldn't he? Whatever he and Sorcha had had between them was over—or at least Cesare thought it was. They were not bound by any word or convention. No promises had been made, nor vows.

The clap of thunder was still distant, but loud enough to startle them. The baby began to cry as the candle flames started to dance manically.

'*Caro,* the storm!' said Pia to her husband.

A drop of rain as warm as bathwater and as big as a euro plopped down onto Sorcha's hand.

Pia stood up. 'We must go.'

'Stay,' said Cesare. 'Don't drive in it.'

'If we go now we'll miss it,' said Luca. 'It's miles away.'

'Not that far,' warned Cesare, with a glance skywards.

Another drop of rain fell and one of the candles went out with a little *hiss*—like a villain suddenly disappearing through a trapdoor at the pantomime. And in the urgent scurry with which people began to scramble to their feet Sorcha heard Letizia ask Cesare a question in a low voice.

'*No—va,*' he said to her.

Sorcha was not a betting woman, but she would have staked a fortune on the certainty that Cesare was telling Letizia to go.

Because an unexpected and unwanted guest had turned up?

She said goodbye to them all as the wind began to whip at the tablecloth, but decided to stay behind on the terrace and help Stephan clear the table. At least she could make herself useful—and she wouldn't have to see whether Cesare was kissing Letizia…

Raindrops were thundering onto the wooden table now, napkins and bread were getting sodden, and as she ran back to the table for a return journey she saw a tall, dark figure appear in the doorway. Her sleeve caught a crystal glass and sent it crashing to one of the flagstones, splintering into a hundred glittering shards. She bent down towards it.

'Don't touch it!'

His voice rang out and was caught up by the gathering wind. Sorcha looked up into his face—his dear, beloved face—which was now as hard and as forbidding as granite. His words sounded as if they were little bits of the stone he had chipped off and flung at her.

He strode over to her and caught her by the wrists, but it was an unequivocal capture—there was no tenderness or softness as his fingers bit into her flesh.

'And now you'd better start giving me some kind of explanation!' he ordered.

CHAPTER THIRTEEN

SORCHA stared at Cesare as the rain came down in great sheets and lashed across their faces, but he didn't seem to be aware of the weather—nor of the fact that if he hadn't been gripping her wrists she might have fallen.

All she could see was the whiteness which had appeared beneath his olive skin, and the way the rain-drops had made his eyelashes into little points, so that his eyes looked like dark stars. But there was no smile nor welcome on his face, just the glitter of accusation and of challenge.

'Well?' he demanded, when she did not answer him.

Her breath was coming in shuddering and painful gulps, and the clouds of jealousy which threatened to engulf her were darker than the stormclouds which were hurling down their contents. She thought about what might have happened if she hadn't turned up here tonight and she felt faint. 'Were you going to sleep with her?' she moaned.

His fingers gripped her even tighter. 'Who?'

'Who? *Who?* Letizia, of course!'

Cesare's eyes narrowed, and suddenly he wanted to hit out at her—to hurt her back as she had hurt him, and maybe make these feelings go away. The world was a dull and predictable place without Sorcha, but at least it wasn't full of pain, of torment and uncertainty.

'What *right* do you think you have,' he flared, and even though the rain was striking his face like hammer-blows he barely felt it, 'to just turn up here *out of the blue* and ask me questions like that?'

Right? No right at all. She should have done that thing people always recommended when you went to see a doctor—writing all your questions down in some coherent sort of order to avoid wasting time by saying the wrong thing or making a fool of yourself. And yet the question had released something—it was like loosening some dark, dank floodgate which, once open, couldn't be shut again.

All she could feel was the deluge of raindrops as they thundered down onto the terrace, and the beating of her heart and the terrible wrench of pain there. 'Would you have done?' she whispered.

Her words were lost in the storm, but he read them as they were framed by her trembling lips and he hauled her inside, into the dry, where their bodies dripped water into puddles which lay on the wooden floor.

'Nothing has happened between Letizia and me. But what do you want me to say?' he demanded. 'That the thought of sleeping with her hadn't crossed my mind? Then I'd be lying! That she isn't ready and willing to? Then I'd also be lying! Or that I am going to spend the rest of my life in celibacy because I could never seem to get it right with you? Well, that would be the biggest lie of all, Sorcha.'

Red-hot anguish caught her by the throat so that her words came out like a torrent of lava. 'Maybe I want you to lie!'

He laughed, but it was a mirthless and bitter sound. 'That is, as you say…tough,' he grated. 'There are many things you can say about our relationship—but at least no one can say it wasn't honest.'

She heard the tense he'd used. Past tense. She swayed. It was over.

His black eyes flickered over her, but he didn't loosen his grip. He could feel the rapid thready beat of her pulse beneath the pressure of his fingers. Witch. *Witch*. 'You still haven't told me why you're here.'

And Sorcha knew then that her jealousy—though agonising and very real—was yet another emotional wall she had been trying to hide behind. And wasn't that the mark of a woman who wasn't brave enough to fight for what she wanted?

This wasn't about pride or possession—not any more. And it wasn't about social convention either—about a woman never declaring her feelings for a man before he had indicated his, as if matters of the heart were like some kind of bidding war. This was about telling this man how she really felt about him—because she would never forgive herself if she didn't.

'I'm here because my life seems empty without you.

It's like you lit something in my world and now the light's gone out.' She drew a shuddering breath, because this was the hardest thing of all. To open her heart to him—to leave herself open to the possibility that he might not want her. 'I'm here because I think I love you.'

Cesare stilled, like an animal in the jungle at the dead of night who had heard the sudden rustle of something unknown in the undergrowth. *Love?*

He thought of the times women had declared love for him in the past—but never with that conditional word. I *think* I love you. The word should have made it less believable, and yet somehow it did the exact opposite— for it showed human fragility as well as fearlessness.

He stared at her, at the way her wet hair streamed down around her shoulders, the way her wet dress hugged her body—a water nymph, just like the first time he had ever set eyes on her—and he felt a powerful pull of longing which went bone-deep.

But the barriers he had built around his heart were too high to be toppled by a single word. He lanced her look. 'Maybe you just miss my body the way I miss yours?'

Sorcha licked a raindrop from her lips. Was that bravado she heard lurking behind the mockery of his words? Or was she crediting him with a softness which wasn't really there?

She thought of the eighteen-year-old Cesare in Maceo's photos—of all the hopes and fears in his young face. Of how she'd always thought him strong and invincible and somehow immune to the pain of living.

Maybe he didn't want her. Or maybe he didn't want her on the level of anything deeper than just good sex. But she would never know unless she had the courage to follow this through. Now.

Sorcha's heart was beating painfully as she pulled her hands free from his grip and placed one palm softly against his wet cheek.

The candles on the terrace had long been blown out by the wind, but the darkness was illuminated by a fork of lightning, so that everything in the room was silver and black.

Show him, she thought. Just show him how much you care.

'I think I love you,' she said again, and she put her arms around him.

She felt him stiffen, but he did not move, and she uttered a silent prayer as she held him closer, tightening her arms around his soaking body. Please know that this isn't sexual, she prayed. Know that it's because I love you and I want to cherish you—to comfort and protect you as women have always done with their men—no matter how strong or proud or arrogant they may be.

For a while he just stood there, stiff and unmoving, but gradually he made a little sound in the back of his throat and his arms went round her, like a man who had suddenly caught hold of a lifebelt. But his words contradicted his gesture.

'You have chosen the wrong man,' he said harshly, against her wet hair. 'You know that, don't you?'

Sorcha felt the salt taste of her tears as she shook her head. 'No,' she whispered. 'I don't.'

But Cesare didn't trust the torrent of feelings which holding her like this was threatening to unleash.

'You need to get dry,' he stated matter-of-factly, gently pushing her away from him. 'Come with me.'

Sorcha could have wept as he led her down a long corridor to an old-fashioned bathroom—but what choice did she have other than to go with him and submit to getting dry? She could hardly claim that she would prefer to catch a debilitating chill if only he would *look* at her properly.

He was quiet and absorbed as found her a giant warm towel and gave her one of his T-shirts.

'Put this on,' he said abruptly. 'I'll go and make us some coffee.'

And then he left her, struggling and feeling more than a little foolish as she stripped off her soaking clothes and rubbed the big towel over her shivering flesh. The T-shirt came to halfway down her thighs, and her nakedness beneath it made her feel vulnerable. But she felt vulnerable in other ways too—and the heart was a far less resilient organ than the rest of the body.

She found that he had changed into a dry pair of jeans and was just putting two mugs of coffee onto a tray. He glanced up.

'You look shattered, *cara,*' he said slowly, his voice sounding distant against the still-raging storm.

Their eyes met. Could he read the silent appeal in

hers? Or was he simply choosing to ignore it? And if so—what did that tell her? She had come all the way out here, hadn't she? Her pride would not let her throw herself down and beg him to want her, to offer her something from the heart if he had nothing to give. 'I am pretty shattered,' she agreed.

'Then let's take this through and go to bed.'

His eyes and his voice and his body language indicated nothing other than practicality. If it was emotion she had been praying for, then it looked as if she was going to be disappointed.

She followed him into a bedroom which was darkened by creaking shutters which rocked in the storm, and he drew her down onto the bed and into his arms, covering them both with a blanket.

For a moment Sorcha held her breath, but even though he was holding her close to his warm chest—as if he were shielding her from the elements outside—she still felt as lost as if she were wandering around outside in the storm.

He hadn't told her how he felt about her. He hadn't mentioned anything about whether they had any kind of future—but she told herself that wasn't the reason she had confessed her feelings. She'd said it because she had needed to—and because he'd needed to hear it. Even if they were destined never to be together she knew she would never have forgiven herself if she hadn't.

But her heart ached as they lay there while the wind raged and the storm lashed and the sound of thunder split the sky. Tight in his arms, her head on his shoulder while he stroked her hair, Sorcha stared at the dark shapes around the room until her eyes began to grow tired, and then her eyelids drifted down and she slept.

When she awoke, it took a moment or two for her to remember where she was—and with the calmness of morning came a sense of disbelief. Had she really just flown out here on a whim and told Cesare that she loved him?

She looked at the man in the bed beside her and moved a little. But Cesare was still sleeping. She wriggled away from him but he didn't stir. How ironic it was that she should have longed for so long to sleep with him, and that—when it had finally happened—the reality had been nothing like her dreams. They had shared the same bed with a chasteness which now seemed to mock her.

She went to the bathroom and washed her face and hands, and then, her head and her heart still full of uncertainty, went outside.

In the fresh, rain-washed light of the morning in the aftermath of the wild storm the villa looked exquisite. It was all so very beautiful—and so unexpected.

Sorcha had never imagined that roses could grow close to olive trees—but there were fragrant pale pink roses with water still dripping from their petals as they curved over an arbour which led from the house, and an olive grove glinted silver in the distance. The vineyard lay to the other side of the villa, with its rows upon rows of fruit-laden vines. The grass was green, and so were the huge mountains which provided such a stunning backdrop.

Sorcha felt a lump well up in her throat as she began to walk—because in the clear light of day what had happened yesterday seemed like a strange kind of dream. Almost as if she shouldn't really be here—that she would open her eyes and find herself back in England, putting on a sharp suit and getting ready to go to work.

She clenched her fists by her sides and willed the tears not to spill from her eyes as she stared out at the beautiful Umbrian countryside.

Lazily, Cesare stirred.

He had been having the craziest dream.

He stretched his arms above his head and murmured, and then his eyes snapped open as he turned his head to the empty space beside him and the indentation of where her head had lain on the pillow.

Had he dreamed it?

He sat up in bed and it all came back to him, like a jigsaw taking shape as all the pieces were added. Sorcha turning up in the middle of the dinner party. The storm. The broken glass. Sorcha telling him…

His eyes narrowed.

Sorcha telling him she loved him.

And him doing a pretty passable imitation of a clam.

He found still-damp soap in the bathroom, and the

plastic bag full of her things still outside on the terrace, but of Sorcha there was no sign. He felt the skin-chill of apprehension—even though logic told him she couldn't have gone far. That they were out in the middle of nowhere.

But the logic on which he'd relied all his life suddenly seemed hopelessly inadequate—because Sorcha was strong and resourceful. And proud. Who could have blamed her if she'd decided to walk the few kilometres up the mountain into Panicale, where someone would telephone for a taxi to come out to her? What if she had? *What if she had?*

Unexpectedly, he felt his heart twist with pain.

She had laid her emotions bare for him to see last night—and he had responded with less interest than he might have given to a new business strategy.

Because strategies were safe, and you knew where you were with them—whereas the way she made him feel was…

Scary.

Yet he hadn't given a thought to how *she* must be feeling…to what it must have cost her to come out here like that and tell him what he meant to her. She had made a gesture of humility—stripped away all her pride to tell him how much she cared.

And what had he given her back?

Nothing.

Standing on the terrace, looking down at the silver gleam of the olive groves, he saw something bright moving into his line of vision and his heart missed a beat—because it was Sorcha. Walking towards him, barefooted and wearing a dark T-shirt of his, with her bright hair contrasting against it and cascading down her back, like a beautiful waterfall.

As she grew closer he could see that her eyes were even greener than the lush grass. But they were shadowed with wariness.

'I thought you'd gone,' he said softly as she approached.

'I was…' What? Wondering whether she was in line for the prize of Idiot of the Year. She bit her lip. 'Cesare—'

'I thought you'd gone,' he whispered, and he shook his head like a man who was just emerging into the bright clear day after a subterranean holiday. He reached out and caught her hands in his, turned them over in his palms and looked at them, and then back up at her dazzling emerald eyes.

'I don't know how to do this, Sorcha,' he said softly.

Sorcha's gaze searched his. 'What?'

'To tell you about the emotion you stir up in my soul.' He stared at her, as helpless then as he'd ever felt in his life, and shrugged his shoulders—as if the movement could shift the intolerable weight which lay on them. 'I don't know why.'

She gripped tightly onto his hands, never wanting to let them go. 'Don't you, Cesare? Don't you really?'

He knew what she was doing. On an intellectual side he could see. She wanted him to confront his demons—

to let them out so that they might fly away and torment him no longer. But was it really that simple?

'Tell me,' she whispered, aware of being on fragile ground. One false move and all would be lost.

'People used to pity Maceo and envy me,' he said slowly. 'Because he had come from the slums while I was brought home to a mansion—but you know, Maceo needed nobody's pity. The home he grew up in was a *real* home. With a mother who was there and a father who came home.'

'And you didn't have that?'

He shook his head. 'My father was rich beyond most men's wildest dreams—but it never seemed to be enough. It was as though he needed to go out and earn more and more, to fill some kind of hole that could never be filled.'

And Cesare had done the same, Sorcha recognised. History had repeated itself, as it always did. 'And your mother?'

'Oh, she was very beautiful—and restless. She did not want a world dominated by a baby when her husband was flying all round the globe chasing achievements. She wanted her taste of the high-life, too…'

His voice tailed off and she saw the furrows which deepened his brow. Sorcha drew in a deep breath. It was as if Cesare had drawn the outline of a picture, and now he needed her help to colour it in. And if they were to be a couple, then that was what couples did, wasn't it? They helped one another. They were there for one another. They laid feelings on the line because those feelings mattered—they didn't pussyfoot around or worry about how it might look, or whether they would be hurt.

'She wasn't there for you?' she said.

He nodded, sensing that it was not censure he heard in her voice, but a fair evaluation of the facts. And in confronting those facts he found they somehow assumed less dominance, less power to hurt. 'No, she wasn't there. There were other people to care for me, but it wasn't the same.' He drew in a deep, shuddering breath as he did the unthinkable and confronted his past head-on. 'Maybe that's why it isn't easy for me to show…love,' he said shakily, and gave her a look like a lost little boy. 'Because I haven't had much practice.'

Sorcha stilled. 'Cesare?' she said breathlessly.

He stared down at her. 'I really thought you'd gone when I woke up this morning.'

Her eyes were still wary. She looked into his face— but she wasn't a mind-reader, and she wasn't going to second-guess him for the rest of her life.

'Do you *want* me to go?'

'Go?' He lifted her hand to his mouth and kissed each fingertip in turn, his eyes never leaving her face. 'I never want you to go away again, *cara mia,* because I think I love you, too. And I really must kiss you now.'

It was the first time he had kissed her in his native land, and it was quite unlike any other kiss they'd ever had—for it was a declaration and a seal, a farewell to past misunderstandings and a celebration of all that lay ahead of them.

When it was over, Sorcha bit back the tears which were shimmering in her eyes as she saw all the possible obstacles in their way. 'But how will we work it, Cesare? How can we be together?'

'Somehow,' he promised. 'We can live here—or in England. We *could* live apart, but I don't want that.'

'Me neither.'

His arms tightened around her, and for the first time Sorcha felt the shimmerings of true physical intimacy.

'Now that I've got you, I never want to let you go,' he whispered. 'The logistics are just details. The important thing is us.'

Us.

Such a tiny word, and yet such a big one—the most important word in any vocabulary—English *or* Italian.

EPILOGUE

A LOOK of pride made his black eyes gleam, and Cesare smiled. 'You look beautiful,' he murmured.

'But you can't see me properly!' Sorcha whispered back with a smile. 'Now, shhh—here's the priest.'

Ivory tulle hung over her face like a creamy waterfall, and the bouquet she carried was of pale pink and frilly roses—the closest match Sorcha could get to those which grew around the Villa Pindaro, where she had found her heart's desire on a clear morning after a mountain storm.

Behind her stood Emma as matron of honour. Her sister was newly pregnant and glowing like a lightbulb, and holding her hand was little Gino who, at the age of four, was deemed old enough to be a pageboy. He was behaving wonderfully—apart from the occasional lapse into solemn thumb-sucking.

Sorcha and Cesare hadn't rushed into marriage—they hadn't felt the need to—and they had made so many big life-changes in order to be together that they wanted to enjoy their wedding in a peaceful state of mind. And you couldn't rush peace of mind.

Sorcha had left England and gone to live in Italy—but it had been no great wrench nor an agonising decision. The world had shrunk and travel was easy, and it had felt like the place she both needed and wanted to be—the place she'd decided they would bring up their children, if they were lucky and blessed enough to have them.

Sorcha had jettisoned her career with the family firm— 'Been there, done that, and wasn't particularly brilliant at it,' as she'd said to Maceo. The corporate rat-race no longer held any appeal. Sometimes you just had to do something in order to get it out of your system.

Instead she had set about becoming competent in the business of running an Italian estate. She had learned about the harvesting of the precious olives and the making of di Arcangelo wine. She'd taken lessons in Italian and grown fluent, and had just started giving English classes to the children in a nearby village.

And Cesare had wound down his corporate life, too. He found that he no longer wanted to restlessly travel the globe, making more money than he would ever need. His life was with Sorcha, and she had built for him the first real home he had ever known. She had shown him how to love, and he had discovered—as with every other thing in his life—that he happened to be exceptionally good at it!

He turned now and smiled tenderly at the woman who would soon be his wife. So far so good. The only flies in the ointment were the banks of paparazzi camped outside the church—but he had only himself to blame for asking Maceo to be his best man!

The Whittaker house was ready for another wedding reception and looking glorious—everything was just about as perfect as it was possible to be. For the first time in his life Cesare was looking forward to the rest of it.

'I love you, Sorcha,' Cesare whispered, just before the priest began to speak.

And Sorcha was glad this wasn't a fairytale, because it would now be ending.

Instead of just beginning.

REQUEST YOUR FREE BOOKS!

HARLEQUIN® *Presents*~

2 FREE NOVELS PLUS 2 FREE GIFTS!

PASSION
GUARANTEED
SEDUCTION

Name	(PLEASE PRINT)

Address	Apt. #

City	State/Prov.	Zip/Postal Code

Signature (if under 18, a parent or guardian must sign)

Mail to the Harlequin Reader Service®:

IN U.S.A.
P.O. Box 1867
Buffalo, NY
14240-1867

IN CANADA
P.O. Box 609
Fort Erie, Ontario
L2A 5X3

Not valid to current Harlequin Presents subscribers.

Want to try two free books from another line?
Call 1-800-873-8635 or visit www.morefreebooks.com.

HP06